THE PROBLEM HORSE

Jenny Hughes

THE PROBLEM HORSE

THE PROBLEM HORSE
Copyright: © 2010 by Jenny Hughes
Original title: The Problem Horse
Cover and inside illustrations: © Asbjørn Tønnesen
Cover layout: Stabenfeldt AS

Typeset by Roberta L. Melzl
Editor: Bobbie Chase
Printed in Germany, 2010

ISBN: 978-1-934983-56-0

Stabenfeldt, Inc.
225 Park Avenue South
New York, NY 10003
www.pony.us

Available exclusively through PONY.

CHAPTER ONE

Jazz once had been a racehorse. His early training had given him wonderful stable manners, the ability to walk calmly along a road in even the heaviest of traffic – and a desire to gallop flat out the moment his hooves touched turf. After riding the 16.2 hands high chestnut Thoroughbred along a quiet country lane and crossing a busy main road, I then trotted him at a brisk working pace up the sloping sandy trail leading to the meadows. Jazz smelled the air with its clean, invigorating tang and I saw a tremor of excitement ripple the muscles under the fine skin of his neck.

"Steady, boy." I kept my voice calm and my hands still, knowing the big horse would sense any tension immediately.

He was perfectly under control, responding

beautifully to my aids, and my aim was to keep him that way. He knew exactly where he was, knew before we crested the hill that before him stretched the glorious sweep of the meadows, miles of mildly undulating turf, a Thoroughbred's idea of pure gallop heaven. He tossed his head, trying to snatch at the bit, the perfect two-time rhythm of trot forgotten as he pranced and rocked, desperate to be off.

"Not till I say so." Staying soft and relaxed, I still refused to let him go, bringing him patiently back to my hands. "Come on Jazz, you know how this works by now."

His big, velvety ears flickered as he listened and gradually he responded, covering the springy turf in a textbook extended trot until I asked for canter. For an instant his handsome nose shot skywards, but I gently brought his head back down and asked again. This time it was a perfect transition, flowing seamlessly into the three beat time of canter, and I marveled yet again at the sheer beauty of his long, free flowing stride. I could see the old man in the distance, sitting astride the square colored cob he chose to ride while he watched us work, his back straight, his hawk-like gaze turned in our direction.

"Keep it just like this, Jazz, and we'll both get a gold star," I said, smiling to myself as we cantered smoothly toward the slight rise where horse and rider surveyed us.

"All right, Tamzin," he called as soon as we were near enough to hear him. "Slow the horse to walk and bring him over to me."

I was pleased to feel Jazz respond immediately and knew I was beaming as we approached the cob. "He's going great, isn't he? What an improvement!"

"Mm." The old man, my grandfather, was never quick to praise. "Not bad, but I want to see him with company. Go down the hill, get one of the others, and canter back to me."

"OK." So far I'd only ridden the chestnut on his own; his re-training program was a slow, painstaking affair of removing his urge to race completely from his day-to-day routine, but I was totally ready for the next stage.

We cantered again, controlled and supple, along the turf trail sloping gently down to where three other riders were schooling their horses in wide, well-trodden circles.

"Hi," I called. "The boss wants someone to canter back with me – any volunteers?"

I have to admit I was really, *really* hoping it would be Seb who responded.

"Sure." To my delight he brought the pure white

warmblood, Challenger, out of the circle and rode over to me. "How's Jazz doing?"

"Great," I tried to look cool. "He's cantering beautifully now; no galloping yet obviously, but Granddad wants to see what he's like with another horse."

"You sure you're all right with that?" The look he gave me made my toes wriggle. "I rode him when he first came here and he's quite a handful."

"I'm fine," I said, giving him what I hoped was my best smile. "Just don't go past him, OK? If he thinks he's in a race I'll never hold him!"

"I wouldn't dream of it and neither would Challenger," he said, patting the stunning gray fondly. "We're both very well-behaved, you know!"

I grinned and moved Jazz closer. "Thanks. I'll start off in trot, OK?"

The two horses moved away together, Jazz's chestnut-colored nose slightly ahead of Challenger's silvery one. Again I could see the skin ripple as his muscles twitched with excitement, but he remembered everything we'd taught him and stayed obediently at trot until I sat for a beat and asked for canter. Seb, his long, lean body curved slightly forward in Challenger's saddle as he watched me, did the same. As soon as Jazz felt the other horse's pace increase he threw up his head in a by now familiar gesture.

"Steady," I said, bringing his nose down, but he fought me, his smooth canter abandoned as his racing instinct took over.

The memory of the first time I rode him flashed briefly into my mind, the terrifying way that he'd plunged into gallop without warning, running blindly, mindlessly across a field, not looking or caring where he was headed. With his formidable weight and strength leaning hard on the bit I stood no chance of stopping him and he'd finally brought himself to a halt by blundering into a hedge, throwing me onto the (luckily soft!) ground. Seb, too, had experienced Jazz's sudden powerful lunge and I heard anxiety in his voice as he said, "Don't let him get away from you, Tamzin."

There was no time for subtlety; the only way to curb Jazz's frightening habit was to prevent it. I managed to keep my voice calm and my body language soft, persuading the big horse to return his pace to a controlled canter. Seb kept Challenger alongside instead of inching ahead, which Jazz would interpret as an invitation to race, or hanging back, which would make the hyper Thoroughbred think of winning.

"Good boy, Jazz," I said quietly. "See, it doesn't have to be a race all the time. This can be fun too."

I felt him relax the muscles he'd bunched, ready for

flight, and softened my hands, smiling as he settled into the beautiful cantering rhythm.

"That's fantastic," Seb's voice was warm and there was a glow of real admiration in the blue eyes looking across at me. "I know just how strong he is and you're so tiny – I don't know how you do it!"

"Jazz is a great horse," I said. "He's just been allowed to develop a bad habit; he doesn't *mean* to be bad."

"Maybe, but I still think you're amazing – oh, there's the boss. I hope he thinks so too."

"If I'm lucky he'll tell me I didn't do too badly," I grinned, looking ahead to where the old man sat watching us. "Granddad doesn't *do* praise."

My grandfather turned his craggy profile toward us, watching with eyes as sharp as they'd ever been.

"Relax your right shoulder, Tamzin," he called. "It's an inch higher than the left."

Feeling the slight shift of weight, Jazz tried to move away. Without putting too much pressure on his mouth I asked him to settle down and he responded at once. Side by side Seb and I brought the two horses down to trot, walking the last few paces before halting directly in front of the piebald cob.

"He still looks very raw compared to Challenger," my granddad said, frowning.

"Challenger is a highly trained show horse," Seb

said, showing his annoyance. "Of course he's going to give a more polished performance than a dumb ex-race horse who's only ever been taught to go flat-out in one direction!"

Although it was kind of nice the way he leaped to my defense, I really wished he hadn't.

"It's OK, Seb," I said. "Uh – yes, Granddad, there's still quite a way to go with Jazz but he's definitely improving."

"Mm," he retorted, looking at the flecks of sweat on the chestnut horse's neck. "He still works himself into a lather trying to get away, doesn't he? I think the owner will have to leave him with us a while longer yet."

"She really loves him," I patted Jazz's shoulder. "She was on the phone again last night asking how he was and if he misses her."

"I hope you told her he's a horse, not a pet poodle." The keen old eyes swiveled. "Challenger's looking pretty good. Fit enough for show training, I'd say."

"Yeah," Seb said, still annoyed.

"Excuse me?" My grandfather raised his eyebrows.

"Yes, Mr. Raynor," Seb said with irony in his voice, but the old man chose to ignore it. "Go on, then, take them back. One more canter, and don't let Jazz snatch the bit this time."

"Yes, Mr. Raynor," Seb said again and I nodded as we walked away.

"Yes, Mr. Raynor," Seb repeated the words sarcastically. "It's worse than being back at school!"

"It's just his way," I tried to explain, hoping to lighten his mood. "He's a little old-fashioned about things like that."

"A little!" Seb shook his head. "It's like he's a hundred years behind the times."

"No he isn't," I said, laughing. "He just has strict ideas about the way to run his business. And you've got to admit Highfields is *the* best there is."

"Yeah, it is terrific," Seb agreed, the gleam returning to his blue eyes. "I never wanted to work anywhere else when I left school and I still can't believe I'm here sometimes, but 'the Boss' does drive me crazy sometimes."

"Oh, me too." I laughed and he looked at me curiously.

"So, will you work here full time? When you finish school, I mean? You're only fourteen now, right?"

"Nearly fifteen," I said swiftly. "And yeah, I guess so. I love horses and I love Highfields, so why not? Will you be – um – staying?"

"Yeah, I hope so. I love the work; it's just that some of the methods aren't exactly what I'd do. When I was young I wanted to be a top rider, but now I'm really interested in training."

"Duh! Anyone would think you were eighty instead of only twenty," I teased him.

He grinned ruefully. "I'm pretty ancient compared to you, and you're already a better rider."

"There are only a few years between us," I pointed out sharply. "But thanks for the compliment. Now, shall we do that canter Granddad asked for?"

"OK," he said, and he got Challenger on the bit and brought him close to Jazz and me. "But be careful – that's one heck of a horse you're riding and you're so small –"

"Yeah, yeah, whatever," I stuck my tongue out at him as I moved the chestnut up through his paces. "Stop saying that – it's *boring*."

His teeth flashed a gorgeous grin, making it hard for me to focus my attention on controlling Jazz. Although I was being perkily joking with Seb, my irritation had an underlying truth. I really *was* fed up with his constant references to my age and size.

I'm not *much* younger than he, and OK, I'm not the tallest girl in the world, I thought grumpily, but Seb treats me like a kid because I'm a few years younger and a bit shorter than he is. It's just not fair!

Jazz, probably sensing my mood, played up, doing his best to run off with me, but I refused to let him get away and at last he settled down so we could both enjoy the canter along a gently sloping trail. Seb and I stopped at the top to enjoy the view, and then took the horses home at a cooling down walk, with Seb chatting easily all the way. Back at the Highfields yard I led Jazz into his roomy box, took off his tack and brushed him down. He always enjoyed the contact and stood like an angel while I checked his hooves and ran my hand over his fine, strong legs to check them. When I gave him a final pat and prepared to leave he nuzzled against me, running soft lips across my palm and nudging me gently.

"You're looking for a treat, aren't you?" I said, scratching his shoulder affectionately. "Sorry, Jazz, I can't give you anything. It's against the rules."

"His owner probably gives him a piece of apple or carrot," Seb's face appeared at the stable door. "It does no harm."

"Granddad doesn't like the habit. He says it encourages horses to nip."

"Jazz doesn't know *how* to nip," Seb scoffed. "The old man's too rigid. Guidelines are fine, but I think we should be flexible, treat each horse as an individual."

"Maybe," I shrugged. "But don't argue with *me* about it."

"I'm not," he said, giving me that sudden, disarming grin. "*You're* a little gem, isn't she, Jazz?"

Whistling he went off to the tack room and I gritted my teeth as I buried my face briefly into the warm chestnut neck. "It's that word again! When will he realize I'm not so little anymore?"

Jazz nuzzled my hair and I hugged him, feeling a strong wave of sadness wash over me. To any pony-crazy outsider my life probably looked perfect – days spent riding beautiful horses like this with company as good-looking and charismatic as Seb – but I knew the reality. As much as I loved the riding I dared not let myself get too attached to Jazz and the other horses because they all had owners and would all, eventually, return to them. There were times, and this was one of them, when I'd gladly swap the glorious setting of Highfields for a modest little stable where I could visit just one pony, who was my own, my very own. I'd love him and pet him and we'd be together every single day and –

"Tamzin!" It was my mom's voice. "Come on, Poppy's waiting for her exercise."

Shaking my head to clear it, I left Jazz's box, storing his saddle neatly in the tack room before selecting the next horse's tack. No matter how sad I was feeling, life at Highfields went on, and hey, so what if the guy I thought was fabulous didn't feel the same way about me? I had a job to do and there were always horses, even though they were other people's horses!

16

CHAPTER TWO

The field mud freshly brushed from her soft bay coat, Poppy gave me a whicker of recognition when I went to fetch her and my mood, as always, lifted immediately. I spoke to her, moving my fingers along her spine and rubbing gently on the patch of white hairs behind her withers. Poppy was another sweetie. A small sturdy mare, she was slightly overweight and pretty ordinary looking, and she'd been a trusted and well-loved family pony for many years. Then, with the youngest child just learning to ride, Poppy had started bucking. Not playful, showing-off bucks, or vicious explosions of bad temper, but they got worse till eventually the young child was badly thrown and the family decided that Poppy would have to go.

Thankfully, they contacted Highfields first and my

mom and granddad were able to tell them what had gone wrong almost immediately. They'd bought the pony a new saddle, not realizing it didn't fit properly and that poor Poppy went through agony every time she was ridden as the front of it dug into her back. Mom had gotten her a well-fitting new one, but by now the mare associated everything cinched onto her with pain and she continued to buck. Her back was no longer sore, and the injured spot had completely healed, although the hair had grown back white instead of brown. Poppy wasn't worried about being ridden. She was perfectly behaved barebacked, but still reacted like a rodeo horse as soon as anyone settled into the feared saddle, so the Highfields' job was to gradually reintroduce the hated piece of tack and reunite the family with their 100% trustworthy pony. Today, for the first time, we were trying her with a numnah, a soft, padded cloth held in place with a broad, comfortable length of webbing.

"She put her ears back when I did up the girth," Mom told me as I led Poppy toward the fenced ring. "So just rest your weight over her back before even attempting to sit on her."

The little mare was anxious, stamping her feet as I gradually leaned across her. It was a slow, patient job and we spent a long time walking her around the ring with me gradually increasing the amount of weight I was putting on her. When Mom gauged the time was right I slid carefully onto the round little back, lowering myself gently, gently onto the numnah. Poppy stopped for an instant, but before she could tense her muscles to buck Mom praised her extravagantly and I slid smoothly back off. Half an hour later I was able to stay aboard for ten minutes and the troubled expression was gone from Poppy's eyes as she stepped out confidently, ears pricked forward. It was nowhere near as exciting as thundering across the meadows on Jazz but I felt the same thrill of achievement and gave the little pony a ton of praise before brushing her down and taking her back to her field.

"Excellent," Mom said with satisfaction as I returned the pony's halter to its hook. "We'll gradually increase the time and pace using the numnah with Poppy, until –"

A bell shrilled loudly across the yard and she looked at her watch. "That'll be the new student. Go and welcome her, will you, Tamzin? I've got the vet coming to examine a new horse."

"OK," I said and started off toward the house where visitors were directed to stop before entering Highfields' ring area.

It's a nice old house, a bit big now that there are just

the three of us, but I can't imagine living anywhere else. It's been in Granddad's family for years, built on a slight elevation so you can see the fields and stables, indoor and outdoor rings, and surrounding countryside from every one of its windows. As I walked I looked around, hoping to see Seb, and then realized he'd be in the indoor ring with Granddad, working on the students' lessons. We already had six this time, the most we usually took, but evidently another one had been accepted. The visitor's bell clanged again as I pushed the garden gate open, making me hurry toward the front door. Leaning theatrically against it, her fingers still pressed on the bell, was a girl of about nineteen or so. She was tall and willowy, dressed in such immaculate riding clothes that I was suddenly uncomfortably aware of the ratty old breeches I wore and the fact that I probably had straw in my dark, straight hair. *Her* hair was gorgeous, a mass of rippling blonde waves, and the face that turned toward me was extremely pretty.

"I was starting to wonder where everyone was," her voice was petulant.

"Sorry. We're all working," I held out my hand as I'd been taught. "I'm Tamzin Raynor."

She touched it briefly with long, manicured fingers. "Sophie Webster. New student. You're not Barney Raynor's daughter, surely?"

"He's my grandfather," I was surprised she'd said Barney and not Mr. Raynor. "He's in the indoor ring supervising lessons. I'll take you there."

"Straight to work, eh? I heard Highfields was run pretty strictly," she said and tossed back her hair.

"You – uh – might want to tie that back," I suggested diffidently. "The boss won't let you ride with it loose like that."

"We'll see." Carrying her riding hat, she followed me through the garden and across the yard.

I stopped outside the ring. "The other students are in there with Seb and my granddad. Do you want me to take you in?"

"No thanks, Tamzin," she gave a sudden, charming smile. "I can introduce myself."

Watching her sashay through the big doors I found myself intrigued to see the Boss's reaction to this stylish new addition, so I moved just inside, positioning myself for a clear view of the class. The students were being put through their paces by Seb, who stood in the center of the ring. Granddad, his back to me, was talking to the group and only Seb heard Sophie's arrival. He turned to watch her approach and to my dismay I saw an expression of besotted delight spread across his good-looking face. Sophie, moving like a model on a catwalk, held out her hand and Seb practically fell over reaching out to shake it. He stammered something and I heard her give a musical trill of laughter in return, making him color up like a dumbstruck schoolboy. My grandfather called Sophie over to him and I stared in disbelief as Seb's eyes followed every slinky move she made.

I'd had a crush on Seb for what seemed like forever, from the moment he'd arrived at Highfields as just one of the students, but until now I hadn't realized how much I'd let it get to me. I was a little jealous, of course; jealous of Sophie's glamorous, nineteen-year-old looks, but mostly of the effect they'd had on Seb, who never stammered or went red when *I* spoke to him. I wanted to get away, to throw my arms around a warm, loving friend who'd listen without telling me not to be silly, I was only a kid. I don't think I'd ever wanted a horse of my own as much as I did at that very moment; one I could love forever, one who wouldn't be leaving in months or even weeks.

"Tamzin!" My mom's face appeared at one of the stable doors. "Quick, I need some help."

I brushed a hand fiercely across my face to warn the tears not to start flowing and went in. Inside the box cowered a roan mare, ears flat back and eyes rolling in terror.

"She won't let me near her," Mom said. "The vet said to sedate her but I don't want to do that."

"What's she so scared of?" I shut the door quietly.

"Everything, I think, but she went completely berserk when Chas tried to touch her head, and nearly flattened him against the wall. Don't go too near in case she tramples you."

I looked at the poor, terrified horse and pushed my own worries away. "It's OK, baby, I won't hurt you."

She blinked and dropped her head slightly.

"That's better," I told her softly. "What's her story, Mom?"

"Her name's Rosa, she's five years old and her owners found their groom beating her one day. They told me it had made her head-shy, which I was sure we could cure, but I didn't know she was this bad."

"I'll stay with her for a while," I said.

"She does seem to like your voice," Mom was still very concerned. "But don't try to touch her. She reacts so violently."

"I won't," I said and leaned against the wall. "I'll just be company for you, won't I, Rosa?"

We stayed there, the roan horse and I, for over an hour with me talking quietly and her listening. Although she spooked at the odd sound coming from outside, gradually, almost imperceptibly, she relaxed, the bunched muscles unknotting, the tense lines of neck and jaw softening. I made no attempt to get nearer, but when she finally took a step forward to take a long drink from her water I felt that a small breakthrough had been made. The sweat patches that had broken out all over her body were beginning to dry and her ears, though twitching nervously, were no longer clamped back as I slid silently out of the box. Having checked my watch I knew the class of students would soon be returning to the yard and wanted to know if Mom intended keeping the petrified mare in the stable with all the noise of voices and clattering horses to scare her again.

To be honest, I also didn't want to be around Seb and Sophie, at least not until I'd gotten myself together. I knew Mom would be in the outdoor ring with one of the other of the horses sent to us for re-schooling, so I went there. At Highfields, Mom is mainly responsible for the horses while Granddad concentrates on the students. Mom's main helper is a vastly experienced old groom named Chas, while Seb, the former student, now works full time as "the Boss's" assistant. Chas was leaning on the ring's fence, watching Mom lunge a piebald cob.

"Hiyah," I greeted him. "I need to find out what we should do with Rosa."

"Send her back home, I should think." His wrinkly face creased even further. "She's a hopeless case, that one. Nearly broke my arm slamming herself against the wall earlier."

"I don't think she meant to. She's scared but I don't think she's *bad*," I said earnestly.

"You and your mom don't think *any* horse is bad," he snorted.

"And we're right; it's people who are the problem, not their horses."

Mom came over and smiled at me. "How's Rosa doing?"

"She's still flinching at every sound. I think she should spend a few days out in a quiet field to help her calm down."

"Good idea. The difficulty will be putting a lead rope on her to get her there. She goes bonkers if you try to touch her head."

"Maybe she'll follow Meg," I suggested. "I think we should try because the students will be in the yard soon and Rosa will hate the racket they make."

"OK," Mom said and handed the lunge rein to Chas. "Will you keep going with the piebald while we take care of this, please? Go and fetch Meg first, Tamzin."

Meg used to be my father's horse. She's well over twenty now and retired from work but she earns her keep as companion and nursemaid, Granddad says. It's always easy to bring her in from the field, so as usual I just stood at the gate and called her. She lifted her old head immediately and, leaving Poppy and the others grazing, walked straight to me. I fastened on a head collar, though she hardly needs one, and led her back to the yard where Mom was waiting. Rosa was again huddled in the back of the stable but her ears flicked forward when she heard my voice, and when Meg put her kindly bay head over the door the roan mare actually took two steps toward us.

"Well done," Mom whispered. "When she saw me with the lead rope she shook all over and backed up into the corner again, so this is great."

"I'll go in." Stepping inside I murmured soft words of encouragement to the frightened horse, making sure I kept my hands at my side. Meg gave a whicker of greeting and Rosa answered with a high-pitched nervous whinny.

"I think she'll follow us," I said. "I'll walk with Meg and I bet Rosa will stay beside her."

"No way," Mom said. "She'll take off."

"I don't think so." I could see something in the roan mare's eyes, a pleading, a recognition. "She needs a friend and Meg's really good at that."

"I suppose she can't get far if she does run, and I can't see her letting us put a halter on her." She stepped back and I slowly opened the door, turning Meg as I did so.

Rosa gave a squeal, a heartbreaking sound I was sure meant, "Don't leave me!"

"Come on, Rosa," I still didn't raise my hand. "Walk on, come with us."

The poor horse's legs were still trembling as she came out of the stable, and I moved Meg forward immediately, not giving Rosa any time to consider bolting. She followed us at once, her soft nose almost touching the bay mare's side. I kept speaking quiet, muted nonsense, telling Rosa what a brave and clever girl she was and that wonderful Meg would be looking after her. Mom, I knew, was poised behind us, ready for any possible trouble. With the two horses at my side I walked past the big field containing Poppy and the others and kept going along the long length of its fence. Rosa stuck to Meg's side like glue and when we reached the gate of our smallest field, the one tucked away from sight of house or yard, she stopped while the bay mare waited politely for me to open it. I led Meg inside, walking a good way into the paddock so that Mom could easily close the gate behind us.

"Good girl, Meggie," I patted and hugged the old horse and she nudged me in a friendly fashion. "You're being a nursemaid for a few days," I told her. "So look after Rosa, she's had a bad time."

The roan horse was still very close, but she backed off while I removed Meg's head collar.

"It's OK," I told her. "I'm not going to touch *you*. You're going to have a vacation to help you forget what happened to you. I'll come over later to make sure you're all right."

She stared at me, her big, dark eyes still filled with anxiety, but there was something else. A connection had been made between us. Meg gave her a nudge and started walking away and Rosa, as if she couldn't believe her luck, followed, moving freely across the open space as if in a dream.

CHAPTER THREE

"Are you OK, Tamzin?" Mom looked at me as we walked back to the yard. "I hope you're not letting Rosa's problems get to you."

We're really close, my mom and I, but I just couldn't tell her how I was feeling about Seb. She knew I liked him, maybe even guessed I had a bit of a crush of him, but I didn't want her to know what an idiot I was being about his reaction to the gorgeous Sophie.

"I – uh – I'm hoping being with Meg will help make her feel better," I said, preferring to stick to the subject of horses. "Rosa looks as though she could do with a break."

"She certainly does. There's an awful lot of work ahead for us but as you say, some quality time with a kind horse friend will do her a world of good before we start."

"Just as well Meg's got something useful to do anyway." The black mood I was in colored everything. "Or Granddad would be thinking of getting rid of her."

"Don't you believe it," she said, putting her arm around me in a hug. "Your granddad wouldn't dream of parting with Meg."

"Oh yeah?" I said sarcastically. "How come he's always saying horses have to earn their keep, then? According to him they only stay if they work."

"Well yes, he thinks all horses should be trained to be useful. Treated properly, they love to please us, and he doesn't like the idea of a lazy pet eating its head off in an owner's field, but Meg – Meg is different. Apart from us two she's the only link Granddad has with his son."

"Dad?" I was taken by surprise. My grandfather so rarely so rarely spoke of him. "He keeps Meg because she used to belong to my dad?"

"Definitely, though he's so used to acting like a heartless old grouch, he probably won't admit it. He keeps his grief private but it goes very deep. Losing Carl changed him a lot. He's actually not the ogre he pretends to be, you know."

"Oh I'm used to his strictness, and anyway he's totally fair," I said, always eager to hear more about the father I could barely remember. "Was Dad like that too?"

"He was," she said, her eyes softening. "Scrupulously fair and hard working – but he was oh, such a lot of fun as well. Highfields was a much happier place when he was around. It's been nearly ten years but I still miss him so much and so does your granddad."

"And me," I felt very emotional. "Even though I was only five when he died."

"I'm glad you remember him that way," she spoke softly.

"Maybe we could go through the photos again tonight," I suggested. "I want to look at the pictures of him riding Meg."

"OK," she said and made a visible effort to return to everyday stuff. "We'll do it after my lesson. I meant to ask you what the new student was like."

I tried to keep my expression neutral. "She seemed OK. How come she's only just turned up? The others started a week ago and there are six of them already."

"I know, Granddad doesn't usually take more than that, but Sophie's a special case. Her dad designed the website and all those clever links for the horse welfare project Granddad was involved with a couple of years ago. He was tremendously helpful. The system would never have worked without him and Granddad was very grateful."

"I can imagine." I smiled at the thought. "Granddad's brilliant when it comes to horses but he still treats computers as though they're from outer space. So, is he returning the favor by letting Sophie join this class?"

"Yes. The poor girl's been through some kind of trauma and wanted to get away. She's an excellent rider, so where better than Highfields?"

Great, I thought gloomily. Seb's already blown away by this girl so when he finds out she's had a tough time he'll be all caring and protective.

"Are you sure you're all right?" Mom shot me another concerned glance. "You seem, I don't know, subdued."

I managed a smile. "I'm fine. Do you want me to take care of the field horses?"

All the horses here spend at least part of every day out in the paddocks, free to wander at will and indulge in some totally natural behavior.

"No thanks." She leaned over and ruffled my hair. "You're on another planet today, aren't you? Chas will do that; you're due to help with my demonstration."

I bit my lip. The last thing I wanted at the moment was contact with Seb and Sophie, but Mom was right; I always assisted with her initial input at the start of a student course. Apart from the blonde girl they'd been here for a week and Granddad liked Mom to give a short lecture at this point. As I said, she doesn't do much of the actual riding technique teaching but she's great at understanding how horses' brains work, providing another insight into the wonderful world of equitation for the students.

Once they'd finished making their horses comfortable and completed their stable chores the group gathered at the outdoor ring, perching comfortably on the fence to watch and listen.

Given the despondent mood I was in, it failed to surprise me that Seb, although he knew the format nearly as well as we did, had also decided to attend and – what do you know – he was sitting right next to Sophie! She'd tied her great, golden mane neatly back for the riding lesson but was now unbraiding it, flirtatiously aware of the effect she was having, not just on Seb, but on most of the other guys too. I led Callie, a pretty dapple-gray part-Arab mare, into the ring and stood quietly next to her, my eyes fixed (pretty sulkily) on the ground. I usually enjoy Mom's little introductory talk. She keeps it short and entertaining but it always gives each new batch of students a lot to think about and it's interesting seeing their reactions. While I stood back she started by loose schooling Callie, getting the mare moving around the ring and obeying her voice commands. Then she asked for comments on the way Callie responded, her cadence, balance and pace.

"Good," she smiled at a very tall, very dark and

quite handsome nineteen-year-old named Leo. "You're starting to *look* now. Later, when we return Callie to the field, I want you all to note the difference in the way she moves when released. In fact, whenever you have any spare time, use it by watching any horse you can when he's moving freely and unrestrained. Even the plainest pony under saddle will amaze you with his grace and beauty when you're not on his back."

There was a murmur within the group and Leo said something that made a couple of them laugh. I wouldn't look at Seb, not wanting to see that besotted glow in his eyes when he gazed at Sophie. The next stage, after Callie had neatly performed several circuits of the ring, was for me to ride her. She stood beautifully and Mom pointed out how she'd correctly balanced and aligned herself as I began to mount. With Mom describing exactly what the mare was experiencing as I sprang lightly from the ground and lowered myself gently into the saddle. Having performed the routine lots of times before, I knew the sequence by heart and sat quietly on the gray mare's back, without using stirrups or reins, while Callie, also a seasoned pro, continued to walk. Mom was teaching the students to observe with their eyes and ears and now pointed out the subtle changes in the horse's movement as she adjusted to my presence. I like hearing the students' comments. They are nearly always experienced riders with a good knowledge of all things equine, but Mom shows them how to be aware of and interpret a horse's body language. This group obviously hadn't given this aspect of riding much thought and got quite excited as the demonstration continued. By the time Callie and I were cantering smoothly around the ring their comments were coming in fast. Chas had set up a couple of small jumps and when, still without reins or stirrups, I rode Callie toward them they all watched intently.

"You'll see how Callie keeps responding to my voice without her rider using any kind of aid, natural or artificial. The horse is as receptive to my voice as she was when being schooled because Tamzin, with a perfect seat and balance, isn't interfering with the horse's comfort and confidence."

"I think I speak for all the guys when I say how much we've been admiring Tamzin's perfect seat," Leo said.

Concentrating on keeping still, I didn't look at him but I could hear the wicked grin in his voice and so, obviously, did my mom.

"Thank you, Leo," she said smoothly. "In which case I'd be obliged if I could use you as a volunteer."

"Helping Tamzin?" He jumped down from the fence as Mom brought Callie to a halt. "Oh yes, *please*."

I felt color flooding into my face as I dismounted but I couldn't help smiling at Leo, who was now making a sweeping bow.

"The boss says you're not a bad rider, Leo," my mom said, smiling too. "So it shouldn't be any trouble for you to do exactly what Tamzin's just shown us."

"Sure, no problem," he said and turned the stirrup iron to face him as he prepared to mount. "Though I can't possibly look as cute as she does."

I blushed again and Mom said briskly, "Don't worry; I'm sure you'll entertain us in other ways."

As soon as he lowered himself into the saddle there was a marked difference in Callie. She dropped her head and shuffled her weight, too well-schooled to object, but obviously uncomfortable.

"What am I doing wrong?" Leo looked surprised.

"Your hips aren't completely square with the horse's hips," Mom said crisply. "And your weight isn't being carried equally on both seat bones, making Callie aware that your thighs and knees aren't properly relaxed. This has upset her own balance, because your position is already hampering her."

The jokey smile fading from his face, Leo adjusted his seat and Callie obediently walked forward when asked. The partnership looked OK till the pace increased but then, with Leo doing his best not to bounce around at a no-stirrups trot, Callie started nodding her head violently.

"She's now pretty uncomfortable." Mom's cool commentary made me chuckle. "Compare her gait and head carriage to her previous performance and you'll see –"

"I don't do much of this," Leo interrupted, now looking hugely embarrassed. "I only ever do rising trot – I'll be better in canter."

I grinned as Mom got Callie to pick up the pace. Mane and tail flying, the gray horse took off, but unbalanced and disorientated, and getting no help from her rider, she struck off on the wrong leg, slipping slightly as she leaned into the next bend. Leo, while admittedly *looking* better than he had before, was still completely off-balance himself and stood no chance of staying put, sliding off the saddle in a clumsy, uncoordinated slither to land face down on the sand. Callie, now that she'd shed him, reverted to a smooth, beautiful canter, doing a complete, perfect circuit before Mom brought her to a halt. It looked very, very funny and the other students were rocking with laughter as Leo climbed slowly to his feet. I was looking straight at him and thought for a moment he was going to explode, seeing a gleam of fury in the dark eyes. Brushing himself off, he regained control

and with an obvious effort gave another mock bow in our direction.

"Point made, Mrs. Raynor."

"I think so," Mom agreed cheerfully. "It's a fine thing to be a competent, effective rider, but with just that extra effort and a bit of work on your basic position you can make the experience a better one for your horse."

"Ooh, Leo," Sophie said, still giggling. "You've still got dirt in your hair and you looked like such a dork!"

"Really?" He turned toward her. "Just as well they didn't put *you* up on Callie though, isn't it? The way you ride, the poor horse would be in therapy for a week."

"Hey," Seb glared at him, all muscle and machismo. "There's no need for that."

"You saw her!" Leo, pride badly dented, snarled back. "I might need a little work but it would take at least a miracle to improve Sophie."

"That's enough!" Mom's small but she has great authority. "Personal comments of that kind are not tolerated here. Tamzin, we'll now resume the lesson, please."

I remounted Callie and went through the rest of the routine, illustrating each point Mom made and listening to the comments from the group. Some of the students came with me when I took the dapple-gray mare back to her field, solemnly making notes as they watched her indulge in a good roll and shake before moving off to join her friends. I found myself longing to see Rosa, to spend some time keeping her company while I sorted out my jealous, muddled mind, so I slipped away and began walking toward the far edges of Highfields' land. I nearly turned back when I saw Leo ahead of me, but he spotted me coming and raised a hand lazily in greeting.

"Here she comes, the gorgeous, the amazing, the highly talented and beautiful Tamzin Raynor!"

His voice carried a long way and while I grinned in embarrassment someone else heard it too.

"Give it a rest, will you, Leo!" Seb still sounded mad. "Don't start picking on Tamzin now. You've done enough upsetting Sophie!"

"Can't I pay the lady a compliment when I want to?" Leo squared up to him. They were both tall, and about the same weight and age despite acting like a pair of five-year-olds in the playground. "I'm only telling the truth like I always do. If Prom Queen Sophie can't take criticism she shouldn't be here."

"All criticism from Highfields is constructive – you ripped into her totally unfairly."

"No I didn't," Leo said, managing to sound bored. "It was the truth. Sophie can't ride."

"Yes she can," Seb hesitated. "Look – she didn't want to tell anyone but she's injured, can hardly sit on a horse at the moment without her back going into a spasm. It was really brave of her to turn up at all."

"I don't see the point if it means she can only ride like a novice," Leo said, which was, I suppose, unkind but true.

"That's for the Boss to decide. In the meantime you back off and leave her alone."

I felt hurt that he'd defended so passionately this girl he'd only just met, and started walking away. It hadn't even occurred to him that Leo's flirty comments to me might be genuine. All he was concerned about was protecting Sophie. He was so busy being macho he didn't notice me go, didn't notice me *at all*, and a graphic picture of the pain in the roan mare's eyes surged into my brain. She'd been hurt, far more than I had known, but somehow our distress seemed to have formed an almost tangible bond between us. I kept walking, going faster and faster till I was running, running to the one place in the world I wanted to be – and that was with Rosa.

CHAPTER FOUR

I'd love to be able to say Rosa felt the same way
about me so I could paint a glorious picture of her
galloping toward me in joyful greeting – but life's
not like that. The roan mare, deeply affected by her
previous ill-treatment, was suspicious of everyone and,
fearing any possible handling, hung back nervously
as I approached. Meg, sweet, kind Meg, was always
pleased to see me and stood patiently while I cried into
her warm, fragrant neck. I was feeling very sorry for
myself by now, and bleated on about Seb and Sophie
until even Meg got tired of me.

I watched her move away, then turned hopefully
to look at Rosa. The beautiful roan horse met my
eyes steadily but I could see she was still wary,
poised for flight if I tried to touch her. Instead I

stayed where I was, settling myself down on the
grass while I continued to look and talk to her. She
blinked and dropped her head a little, her pretty ears
pricked forward as if she was really listening. Mom
had said the mare seemed to like my voice so I made
my tone calm and gentle and just kept on talking. It
was amazingly therapeutic, out there in the peaceful
meadow with just the two horses for company. Meg
had returned to her grazing a short distance away but
Rosa gradually moved closer to me as though she
sensed that I needed her. Again we stayed like that
for a long time, by now so close her soft nose was
almost touching my shoulder. I kept my hands very
still and knew my body language was now relaxed,
all the tension I'd built up slowly ebbing away. I
could honestly feel a strengthening bond of empathy
growing between us, and when I finally got to my feet
Rosa, who only hours before had been terrified of all
human contact, stayed by my side. For the first time
I moved my hand, briefly brushing her shoulder with
my fingers, and felt the immediate shudder as her skin
registered my touch.

"It's OK," I said softly. "I'll never hurt you, Rosa.
I promise."

The anxious light in her dark eyes was still there
as I turned to walk away, but as she realized I wasn't

taking her from this new paradise, a warm glow began to shine in its place. Rosa didn't even know she'd had her first lesson with me, but in fact she was learning to trust and I knew just how valuable that was going to be. There was no sign of Seb or Leo as I walked back to the house and I wondered sourly if they'd taken their stupid macho fight somewhere else.

"Hello, love," Mom greeted me as I kicked off my boots at the kitchen door. "Have you only just left Rosa?"

"Yes," I was surprised she knew where I'd been. "You saw us?"

"Yes. I went up to the field to see if she'd let me near her but you were doing so well I left you alone."

"I tried looking in on her while you two were working in the ring," Granddad said, giving me his customary brief smile. "But she took off the minute I went in the field, galloped as far away as she could. She's a good looking mare with a nice action, but whether you can ever get her to trust people again … well, I have my doubts."

"Granddad has his doubts about everything," Mom laughed. "Including the new student."

"Sophie?" Even though I knew it was mean, I hoped he objected to her outrageous flirting and was going to send her home.

"Mm. Apparently Leo's comments were pretty accurate," Mom made a wry face.

"Her dad told me she was a good rider," Granddad grumbled. "Sophie doesn't even sit correctly."

"Ah," I said. Although the jealous side of me would *love* to be rid of the blonde girl, I knew I had to be fair. "She hasn't told you? She was injured recently and her back and is in terrible pain when she tries to ride."

"There you are," Mom said and flipped him lightly with a tea towel. "You should have checked with Tamzin before getting so grumpy about Sophie. Your granddaughter's very well informed!"

"Huh!" The old man was still grouchy. "What's the point of her being here if she's not able to ride properly?"

"Leo said the same thing," I agreed. "But Seb told him it was your decision whether she stayed or not."

"Sophie was so eager she probably couldn't bear the thought of missing out on the course," Mom said understandingly. "Maybe her back will improve, and until it does she could attend the lessons to look, listen and learn."

"I'll see," answered Granddad. Although he made all major decisions concerning Highfields he had a high regard for Mom's opinions. "Though I can't say she struck me as the studious type."

"Seb liked her," Mom had her back to me so didn't notice me wince. "Maybe he could help her. I just hope that cocky devil Leo doesn't stir up trouble. You'll have to keep an eye on him."

"Don't worry, I can always spot a troublemaker," Granddad said as he handed me three plates. "He's a bit too familiar with Tamzin for my liking, as well."

"Familiar?" Mom put a casserole dish on the table. "You mean he flirts with her? Tamzin's a very pretty girl, haven't you noticed?"

"Hey, don't talk about me as if I'm not here," I objected, feeling color rush into my face again. "And don't forget about the photos tonight, will you, Mom?"

"Photos?" Granddad raised his bushy eyebrows.

"Ones of Carl riding Meg," she said briskly.

"Oh," his face became immediately became shuttered and I heard Mom sigh.

It was nice going through the pictures, looking at the tall, handsome man sitting easily astride a younger, fitter Meg, but although Mom answered all my questions and talked lovingly about my dad, Granddad didn't even stay in the room with us.

"He still finds it hard to talk about his son," Mom explained. "Granddad's always bottled up his emotions, but you mustn't think he doesn't have any."

"Mm," I picked up a photo of Dad tackling a cross-country course on the big bay mare. "Meg looks like quite a spitfire here, doesn't she? Yet she's so gentle now."

"She's always had a lovely nature," Mom said and tidied the pictures away. "So don't worry, because I can tell you are. She'll look after your Rosa really well."

"Your Rosa," I repeated the words dreamily as I got ready for bed.

If only the roan mare really *was* mine – if only. I shook my head to clear it. The horse was here to have her problems solved and then, like all the others, she'd return to her *real* owner.

"They've gotten rid of the groom who hurt her," I told myself firmly, "so they're obviously good people and they'll take good care of Rosa once they get her back."

I knew it was hopeless; despite the feeling of connection between Rosa and me she'd never be mine, and the most I could do for her was help her through her fear. I decided to put everything else out of my mind and spend the next few weeks concentrating solely on the beautiful mare. Nothing else, I told myself, nothing else was going to get to me – and I meant every word right up to the moment I walked into the yard next morning and saw Seb gazing adoringly into Sophie's pretty blue eyes!

He didn't even see *me*, didn't notice at all as I slid quietly into Jazz's stable, and again I felt hurt and ignored. I groomed the Thoroughbred, being extra careful of his ticklish spots (he had a lot of those) and tried to rise above the feeling of bitterness that was starting to overwhelm me again. Once Jazz was tacked up and ready for work I led him into the yard, doing my best to not look in Seb's direction. As the Boss's right-hand man he was mainly responsible for riding instruction and show training, usually leaving the stable management to Chas, but I wasn't the least surprised to see him helping the blonde girl with the palomino she'd been told to get ready.

"I'll pick his feet out. It'll hurt your back too much," he said, and the smile he gave her would have buckled my knees.

"Thanks, Seb," she said, obviously used to being looked at like that. "I'm so sorry to be a nuisance."

"I was going to call you a lot worse," Leo said, sounding even more irritated than I felt. "If you can't do any of this stuff, Prom Queen, why don't you clear out of here?"

"Mr. Raynor says I can study from the ground till I'm well enough to ride," Sophie retorted and she glared at him. "*Not* that it's any of your business."

"You're slowing everything down." He pushed past

her and turned his wolfish grin in my direction.
"I want to be as brilliant as Tamzin when I leave here
and you're getting in my way."

"Go and get your horse and leave Sophie alone,"
Seb said, sounding as if he'd like to say something
stronger. "The Boss is already in the ring; you'd better
not keep him waiting."

As I rode Jazz out of the yard the rest of the
students were leading their horses toward the indoor
ring with Seb and Sophie following, her blonde head
very close to his dark one as if she was whispering
in his ear. I wouldn't let myself feel jealous, and just
concentrated on being relaxed, calm and in control of
the big chestnut horse. Jazz was, as always, a pleasure
to ride along the country lane and when we were near
enough to the busy main road to hear the sound of
heavy traffic he didn't waver, but just moved forward
at a beautiful long-striding walk. Whenever I wanted
to dispel the negative vibe about Seb and Sophie my
thoughts turned automatically to Rosa and I wondered
now what she'd be like to ride, like this. As Granddad
had observed, she moved beautifully, indicating she'd
be a real joy, but of course we'd never know unless
we managed to cure her terrible fear of being touched.
I knew that could take a long time. Rebuilding the
confidence of a damaged horse is a long, slow process

and if her owner lost patience ... I couldn't bear thinking about.

"Maybe, if Rosa's owners won't wait for her to improve, *we* could buy her," I said hopefully to Jazz.

He flicked a chestnut ear in response.

"Yeah, you're right," I patted his shoulder gloomily. "Granddad would never agree. Except for Meg, Highfields doesn't keep any horse unless it can do a proper day's work. Poor Rosa can't even bear having her head touched, let alone endure anyone putting a bridle on, so I'd have no chance of persuading him to buy her."

Jazz blew down his nose and I patted him again.

"*You* don't have to worry! Your owner loves you and is totally looking forward to you going home to her. Just remember that when we reach the meadows and don't go bombing off, do you hear?"

As if he'd understood every word the big Thoroughbred was particularly well-behaved, and even with the twin worries of the Sophie-besotted Seb and head-shy Rosa pounding in my brain I still enjoyed the sheer thrill of cantering across the great sweep of land. Jazz didn't throw his head up once to try to snatch the bit, and I thought even the Boss would have been pleased with his performance. As I turned the chestnut toward home, I went through the routine I'd planned for Rosa.

I'd already looked in on her earlier, walking across

the dew-laden grass to make sure she and Meg were OK. Meg greeted me in her usual friendly way and, to my delight, gave Rosa a gentle nudge with her nose as if to say, "Your turn!" The roan mare, her eyes still a little fearful, approached warily, but when I made no move to grab or even touch her she stayed close. I spoke to her softly, just nonsense baby talk, but again she seemed to take pleasure from my voice. This time, when I briefly touched her shoulder, she didn't react with an involuntary shudder of fear. Now that summer vacation had begun I had a lot more time and I planned to spend a big chunk of the afternoon in the secluded field, just letting Rosa get used to having someone around, someone who wasn't going to harm her. A few days like that should produce signs of improvement, at which point we'd bring in someone else for her to get to know. Normally I'd have gone straight to Seb. He was wonderful with nervous horses, and also any time spent with him was something to look forward to, but I was sure there was no point asking now that Sophie was on the scene. As I rode back to Highfields I reflected that no matter how I tried everything seemed to revolve around Seb, so when I heard what sounded like the big daddy of all arguments coming from the yard I was almost resigned to the fact that his voice was right in the middle of it.

CHAPTER FIVE

The fight, as if I hadn't guessed, was between Leo and Seb, with Sophie sobbing noisily behind them.

"Look what you've done!" Seb was bellowing as I slid out of Jazz's saddle and led him toward his stable. "As if Sophie hasn't got enough pain to put up with – now you've made her cry!"

"She's crying because she's a sap," Leo sneered. "Her sore back doesn't seem to keep her from flouncing around the place – it only acts up when she's asked to do some work."

"That's not true," said Sophie. Even with tears in her eyes she still looked pretty. "I did my best but I just can't lift anything heavy."

"You can't ride, you can't even carry a hay net … what's the point of being here?" Leo was standing

53

very close to Sophie, and Seb, like a knight in shining armor, moved between them as if to protect her.

"If you touch her, Leo, I swear I'll –"

"That's enough!" My granddad's voice was like a whiplash. "I will not have fighting in my yard. Leo, get away from those stables and go over to the tack room to help Chas. Sophie, go and write up your notes and Seb – come with me."

I peeped over Jazz's door as they dispersed, looking anxiously at Seb's furious expression and the way he was clenching and unclenching his fists as he followed Granddad. I've nearly always found Seb absolutely great, patient, kind and good-natured but am also aware he has a dark side. A quick, explosive temper he usually keeps well tamped down has flared occasionally, but today it seemed as though he'd completely lost control of it. Granddad just doesn't allow displays of temper, and although he and Seb often disagree about training methods there are never raised voices or physical threats. Such things just aren't tolerated at Highfields. I really, *really* hoped Seb wouldn't mouth off to Granddad. If he started shouting the way he'd been doing at Leo he'd be out of a job, out of Highfields and out of my life.

"Not that *I* can do anything about it," I said, giving Jazz's tail a long sweep with my brush.

"Come on, pal, you're off to the field now. You were so good this morning you've got the rest of the day off, you lucky boy."

Jazz whickered agreeably as I buckled on his head collar and then followed me out eagerly. I led him to the big paddock and released him, watching with pleasure as he sauntered across the grass to join the others grazing in a companionable group a short distance away. The first thing most horses do when you turn them out is to roll, spending several minutes pawing at a chosen spot before lowering themselves onto it for a long, pleasurable squirm, but I'd noticed Jazz always liked to check out his friends first. Rosa, when she'd reached the haven of her field, had simply run, her past experience telling her to get as far away as she could from the source of pain – and that source was people. I vowed again to do everything I possibly could to restore the beautiful horse's faith in humanity, to make her happy again so she could enjoy the natural pleasures horses should be allowed. Jazz was, most certainly, very happy, nuzzling noses with Poppy and then Callie. They were obviously his favorites, and I smiled to see the two mares toss their manes coquettishly as if they were flirting with him. It made me, of course, think of Sophie and the way Seb looked at her when she shook her blonde hair around. I felt my spirits sink as I trudged back to the yard.

"Tamzin!" It was Seb, leaning against a wall, looking sullen.

I approached him reluctantly.

"What's going on?" he asked. He still sounded wound up, but his temper was held in check.

"What do you mean?"

"This thing with Leo. Why's he giving Sophie such a hard time?"

"How should I know?" I thought it was a perfectly reasonable reply but he scowled again.

"You two seem pretty close, I thought he might have told you what his problem is."

Close? What did he mean – close?

"No, he hasn't," I said shortly.

"I thought he was all right," Seb kicked the wall moodily. "Last week, I mean. He was a little cocky but no real trouble. Then Sophie arrives and it's like he can't stand the sight of her."

The thought of *anyone* not liking the gorgeous Sophie seemed completely beyond him.

"The course works better with six people, not seven, and the lessons are slowed down a bit so she can take notes," I said. "A couple of the others, Tina and Kay, were moaning about it too."

"Yeah, OK, I can understand that, but Leo's way over the top, yelling at her and calling her names all the time. Sophie's very sensitive."

Oh, not just blonde and beautiful, but sensitive too!

"I'm sure she is," I kept my voice deliberately flat. "But Granddad won't let Leo bully her, so let him sort it out. You're just making it worse by fighting with him."

"So I've been told," he said, his mouth turned down at the corners, making his usually handsome face look like a sulky mask. "*Mr.* Raynor tells me there's no room at Highfields for aggression. I've been told to curb mine or go."

"I think that's fair." I just wasn't going to show him how much I'd hate it if that happened.

"Oh, thanks for your support, Tamzin," he snapped. "I thought we were friends."

We are, I thought. Only you seem to forget that when Sophie's around.

I didn't say it, of course. I just shrugged and started to move away but he brushed past me angrily, no doubt off to find Sophie and be patient and kind and loving to her. I didn't have anyone to pour out my feelings to and had to control a strong urge to run to Rosa, but of course I couldn't. I had work to do. My next horse was waiting.

Rudy, a spirited liver chestnut, had strong ideas about how he liked to be ridden and had started the scary habit of rearing when he didn't get his own way. At first he only tried this a couple of times in the schooling ring, but his owner sensibly contacted us the day the naughty pony objected to something on a busy road by rearing high on his hind legs. Mom listened carefully to the story and knew this was something we could help with. Rudy had discovered that rearing, something horses do quite naturally especially as youngsters in play, gave him temporary power over his "herd leader," the rider. Our job was to prevent Rudy from rearing in the first place by breaking the pattern he was beginning to establish. Once a horse is allowed to develop a habit it's very hard to cure him, so just as my work on Jazz was designed to stop him from going off at a flat-out gallop whenever he wanted, Mom and I were now going to reeducate Rudy out of his dangerous new game.

Mom's take on this is nice and straightforward, based on the principle that a horse can't do two things at once. If he starts to rear and you switch the action to something else, you'll turn the movement into one you're able to control. I thought it sounded a little complicated when she first explained, but since then I've tried the technique lots of times and it really works. Today Rudy started off nicely, going through his warm-up exercises correctly and progressing to simple wide circles in trot, then canter.

"As soon as you feel him object to anything you ask, get ready to prevent him from rearing by changing his action," Mom instructed from her position in the center of the ring.

She told me the easiest swap was to turn a rear into a spin because both moves start the same way, with the horse rocking back on his hindquarters to lift up in front. Rudy was beginning to fidget and act up, so as soon as I felt him start to rear I did as Mom said. Rudy, busy maneuvering the spin with all four hooves firmly on the ground, was now incapable of rearing. The power to intimidate me was gone and I remained totally in charge. We schooled him for about forty-five minutes, with him trying occasionally to rear and me thwarting him, so that by the end of the session he was accepting every command, interpreting every aid perfectly and generally behaving like the lovely boy he'd been before he discovered the secret weapon of rearing.

"Great," Mom said with satisfaction as I rode out of the ring. "Poppy's next but I don't think Chas has brought her in from the paddock yet."

"I'll get her." I dismounted and handed her Rudy's reins.

Swinging a head collar, I set off for the field again and wouldn't you know it, outside the yard the first person I saw was Seb, again. I nodded briefly at him and kept walking.

"Are you going to see the new mare – Rosa, right?" His voice was still surly but he was patently making an effort.

"No," I didn't want to talk to him.

"I was going to offer to give you a hand."

"Oh," I stopped and looked at him. "Shouldn't you be teaching in the ring?"

"The Boss doesn't want me around at the moment. He seems to think I've got an attitude problem."

"Really?" I said it very sarcastically. "I'd never have guessed."

"Oh, come on Tamzin, don't give me a hard time. Just because you've got a new boyfriend there's no need to ignore me."

I couldn't believe his nerve. "I'm not ignoring you and I don't. Have a boyfriend, I mean."

"Glad to hear it. Leo's bad news. He's ticked off because he knows he wouldn't stand a chance with Sophie and that's the real reason he's so mad at her. Now he's pretending to be after *you* even though you're much too young for him."

"There you go mouthing off about my age again! Even if I *was* with Leo it's got nothing to do with you," I said, feeling red heat rushing to my face. "And as for helping with Rosa – I wouldn't want you and your bad temper anywhere near her."

"That's totally unfair!" He was really snarling. "I might get worked up about people but *never* with horses."

I knew this was completely true but somehow I couldn't bring myself to say it. I just turned away and kept on walking and when I came back with Poppy, Seb was gone. I really, *really* wished I hadn't said that about Rosa, but a combination of hurt and irritation had taken over and it was too late to take it back. I had to work hard to be calm in order to make Poppy's lesson a pleasant experience for her and was rewarded when the little bay relaxed enough to let me sit on the saddle cloth and ride her gently around the ring.

"We're getting there!" Mom was jubilant. "She didn't even think about bucking so it won't be long before we can try her in a saddle."

Because it was a short session Poppy was going to stay in one of the stables for a few hours so we could go through the patient routine again later in the day.

"Little and often," Mom smiled. "Regular and – are you OK, love?"

"Fine," I lied. "Who's next?"

"Chas and I are doing some lunging," she said and looked at her schedule. "You can help or –"

"I'll go and see Rosa," I said immediately and she looked at me.

"That's great, Tamzin. She needs a lot of time spent on her, but I'm worried you're getting too attached. You know the rule."

"Yeah, don't get too fond, they're all someone else's horse." My bitterness was back and Mom looked worried. "It's OK," I said and forced a grin. "I'll treat Rosa like all our other customers."

"She's more of a patient," Mom said. "Not your type, really. It's not riding she needs – it's nursing."

She had a point. I absolutely adore riding and most of my input at Highfields has been doing just that, but despite the fact it was impossible to put a bridle on the roan mare she'd made more impact on me than any other horse I'd known. I was so looking forward to being with her that I broke into a run as I left the yard, but a twinge of conscience made me stop after just a few yards. I'd been unfair to Seb, telling him I didn't want him near Rosa when I knew that actually his gentle approach would be good for her. Seb was already in deep trouble with Granddad over his display of temper, and I figured that at this moment he needed a friend, so I turned back and went to look for him. As I rounded a corner I caught sight of him a short way ahead. His back was turned and as I opened my mouth to call his name I realized he wasn't alone. Sophie was next him, her face raised to his, and I stopped in dismay when I saw Seb moving in closer and closer.

He's going to kiss her! I thought and, as I'd done before when overcome by emotion, I turned and ran straight back to Rosa.

CHAPTER SIX

I was in such a state that I practically threw myself over the gate, clambering onto its top bar to jump down on the grass. Rosa, grazing quietly alongside Meg, raised her head sharply at the clatter and I forced myself to calm down. The last thing this poor shattered horse needed was someone noisy and agitated around her so I took several deep breaths and stood completely still. The roan mare watched me carefully and then, to my utter delight, she began walking toward me. I wanted to run and meet her, to bury myself in her warm, comforting neck and sob loudly that my heart had been broken, but I knew it would scare her off forever.

So I stayed where I was, hands loosely at my sides, taking deep, restorative breaths and waiting until the beautiful horse stopped right in front of me. I spoke her name softly and she brought her velvet nose so close that she was almost touching my face. I breathed in the clover-sweet scent of her breath and kept talking, slowly, slowly moving my hand until I could rest my fingers on her shoulder. She didn't flinch even when I started moving them, closing her eyes with pleasure at the gentle, unthreatening touch. Meg came across to say hello and I petted her with my other hand, making sure my fingers traveled all over her neck and head. She particularly enjoys having her ears rubbed so I did them thoroughly, crooning nonsense the whole time.

"Look at Meg, Rosa! See how much she likes having this done."

I still hadn't gotten higher than the roan mare's shoulder with my other hand, sensing a minute tremor of fear every time my fingers strayed toward her neck. I massaged, scratched and tickled them both for so long my arms started to ache so I slowly brought them down to my sides and waited to see what the two horses would do. Meg blew down her nose and gave me a nudge as if to say, "More, please!" but when I didn't oblige she moved away and peaceably resumed her grazing. Rosa, though, stayed beside me, regarding me solemnly with her big dark eyes. I took a few steps, just ambling across the grass and was thrilled to see her follow. We walked around together for several minutes, me still talking and Rosa listening, her beautiful head in line with my own. It probably doesn't sound like much but it was wonderful, an almost magical experience having her so close, so trusting, so *happy*.

I reached out my hand and touched her shoulder again, and then stretched my fingertips in brief contact with her neck. A faint spasm flickered under her skin but she didn't jerk away. I'd seen my mom handle a head-shy pony many years ago and she had this great trick where she raised her hand so quietly and swiftly she was able to touch his ears and be gone again before he could properly register the contact. She said the technique taught the pony that having his head touched wasn't the torment he'd learned to fear so terribly. This was, of course, exactly what I was trying to convey to Rosa, but I was worried about trying the trick in case I got it wrong and scared her.

"We'll do it the slow way," I said and moved my hand back to her shoulder as soon as her neck muscle stopped twitching. "See, you weren't sure what to think when I did that but I didn't take my hand away till you stopped worrying about it. This is building trust, Rosa, and you're doing very well."

I spent over two hours with her, chatting, stroking and just chilling. I also did some necessary field cleaning so she'd get used to the clatter of the wheelbarrow and fork. In fact she didn't mind that at all and still stayed with me even when I cleaned out the open-fronted field shelter in the corner of the field.

"Thanks, Rosa," I said and stowed the fork and wheelbarrow neatly against the side of the shelter. "That's not one of the fun sides of looking after a horse but having you around made it all right."

We walked back to join Meg, Rosa still moving alongside me as though we were best friends out for a stroll together.

"Which is exactly what we are," I patted Meg. "So, keep looking after my best friend Rosa for me, please, Meggie. She's already a hundred times better than when she arrived."

The roan horse solemnly accompanied me to the gate where I gave her lower neck one last stroke as I said goodbye.

"I'll be back tonight with a little supper for you both," I told her. "Mom will come too so make sure you behave the way you're doing now. She'll be super impressed!"

She stood and watched me leave, not turning back to rejoin Meg until I was out of sight. (I know because I crept back for one more peek at her. Am I a sap or what!) The shock of seeing Seb kissing Sophie had faded; being with Rosa was the best therapy I could wish for. She and I had decided I was going to push all thoughts of Seb away in the future. After all, I'd reasoned to her, he hadn't actually done anything *wrong,* had he? I mean, he was young, free and single. He could fall for anyone he liked and, of course, kiss her. I could accept that I was too young for the kiss to be for me, but it was still tough.

"You look worried," Mom said, coming out of Poppy's stable. "Trouble with Rosa?"

"No, she's doing great," I gave my practiced smile and pushed Seb to the back of my mind. "Absolutely fine. Do you want me to ride Poppy first?"

"Please. She did so well this morning that I've put a heavier numnah on her back. She's stopped panicking when I do the girth up now, so that's another good sign."

The little round mare was still suspicious though, her memory retaining the pain she associated with the ill-fitting saddle, so Mom patiently led her around the ring while I leaned across the numnah. We continued like this for quite a while until Poppy relaxed enough to accept my full weight lying across her back, and only then did Mom give me a leg up. I lowered myself very carefully onto the saddlecloth and sat quietly, being careful not to interfere with her action by giving leg or seat aids. Once she was walking happily Mom handed me the reins and Poppy and I did several circuits in the ring, plus some serpentines and wide circles to add variety. Not once did the bay pony object and I knew we were well on our way to the next step of riding her in a lightweight, proper saddle.

"Although Poppy started to buck in an effort to get rid of the pain the saddle caused, it became a habit," Mom told me. "One she couldn't help even when the cause was removed. We're just re-educating her, helping her to forget about a previous bad experience and go back to being a kind, reliable pony."

"She's a sweetie," I dismounted carefully and gave Poppy a hug. "Not the most exciting horse I've ever ridden but still lovely."

"As lovely as Rosa?" Mom asked slyly.

I smiled, trying not to look sad. "Don't suppose I'll ever sit on Rosa, will I? So I can't compare."

"Mm, a very non-committal answer," Mom looked at her watch. "We're doing well for time so I'd like you to school Rudy one more time before he goes back to the field."

"OK," I said agreeably. "He's doing great, isn't he?"

Riding the liver chestnut was a total contrast and it took a lot of energy and concentration to contain his excitable, effervescent nature. Twice he tried to rear and twice I anticipated the move, successfully maneuvering him into a harmless spin.

"You've got him settled beautifully," Mom called as Rudy and I took the perimeter track of the ring at a perfect controlled canter.

"Oh, just get off my case, will you?" Sophie sounded loud and petulant and from the corner of my eye I saw the golden gleam of her hair as she went storming past the ring fence.

"If you don't do your share of the work it's *my* case too!" Leo, his voice an angry roar, ran after her, and, completely distracted, I turned my head briefly toward them.

Whether startled by the sudden noise they made, or simply sensing that I wasn't concentrating, Rudy reacted instantly with his newfound weapon, rearing up on his hind legs, twisting slightly as he did so. I can't think how I stayed in the saddle. The action was so violent and sudden that I could understand how scared his owner had been. Rudy's head was now way above mine, and his back was almost a straight line as he stood on his hind feet and defiantly pawed the air with his front. Somehow, though, I stayed with him, but the wicked twist he gave made me lose my stirrups, making it very difficult to push my weight forward onto the rearing horse's neck. It was a bit like clinging to the side of a cliff, and the thought that Rudy might just keep going, throwing himself back so far that we both

toppled over, flashed into my mind. I managed to create enough downward pressure to prevent him from going any further and gave silent thanks as his forefeet finally touched ground again. The naughty horse, expecting his protest to have dumped me, was surprised to find me still on board and still in charge, and I moved him immediately into a tight, uncomfortable circle. Rudy, who, as Mom said, could only manage one thing at a time, abandoned any idea of rearing again and meekly obeyed the command. Then after completing the circle he continued in perfect fashion around the ring again.

"Well *done,*" Mom watched me as I brought him to a halt. "I thought he'd lost you with that rodeo act. Just wait till I get hold of Sophie and Leo – it was completely their fault."

"What was?" Seb had just appeared.

"Those two running around screaming at each other nearly caused a nasty accident," Mom was really wound up. "The horse reared and Tamzin could have been badly thrown."

"Tam never falls off. What was the matter with Sophie? Was Leo bullying her again?"

Oh terrific, he's supposed to be my friend, yet when he hears it's his new girlfriend's fault I might have been injured how does he react? By worrying about *her* and not me!

"I have no idea," Mom said impatiently. "But unless they get their conflict resolved they can *both* leave as far as I'm concerned."

I didn't want to see the look of alarm I was sure flared in Seb's eyes as the thought of losing his precious Sophie, so I turned Rudy away and put him through a series of cooling down exercises, concentrating so hard I didn't see Seb go. Rudy was positively angelic, showing no sign at all of objecting to anything I asked, and I thought cynically that maybe part of his problem was being a boy. From my point of view the male sex were giving me nothing but trouble and, again, I couldn't wait to finish the afternoon's session and go back to my darling *girl,* Rosa. Maybe Mom understood that because for once she didn't go on about my becoming too attached.

"I don't blame you," she said when I announced where I was going. "You and Rosa can give each other some TLC. You need it after coping with Rudy."

"It wasn't his fault," I defended the naughty horse. "Well, it was, he shouldn't have reacted by rearing, but —"

"But Sophie and Leo should *definitely* have not made that racket," she pressed her lips together. "And I'm going to make sure it doesn't happen again."

"Mom's mad but it doesn't sound as though she'll make

Granddad throw them out," I told Rosa as, a few minutes later, we took up our now customary position in the field. "Which, to be really honest, is what I wish would happen."

Rosa, her eyes closing blissfully as I gently scratched her neck, gave a small whicker of support.

"But I guess that's just mean of me. Sophie does seem like a bit of a jerk but she hasn't deliberately done anything bad to me and she *is* in pain, after all. She's been through a bad time too, apparently and you know what that's like, don't you, baby?"

My hand crept higher as I spoke and I saw the roan mare flick open one dark eye apprehensively.

"It's OK," I told her. "I know I'm getting pretty close to your head but trust me, it's OK."

The ripple of fear trembled under her skin but I kept going, my fingertips moving imperceptibly up her neck.

"Then there's Leo," I continued, relaying a step-by-step account about the whole story of Rudy's lesson, and as Rosa listened she relaxed again, the twitching muscle in her neck quiet and calm.

"I mean he's a pain as well, a different kind, loud and brash and cocky, but I guess he's genuinely frustrated his lessons aren't progressing as fast as he'd like because of Sophie. He and Sampson, his showy black horse – maybe you've seen him in the field next door? – anyway they're due to enter the competition for the Cavel Cup next month and –"

I'd actually reached the top of the roan mare's neck and she was still letting me pet her.

"Clever girl," I crooned, sliding my hand gently down. "I'll stop now because it's always important to end a lesson on a high note. Bet you didn't even know this was a lesson, did you?"

She opened her beautiful soft eyes and regarded me soulfully.

"I'll do it again in a while," I promised. "And maybe next time you'll be happy to let me touch your head."

She was certainly very happy being with me, accompanying me everywhere I went like an enormous affectionate puppy and listening with the utmost patience to my concerns about Seb.

"He didn't care," I said for about the millionth time. "Not in the slightest. I could have had a terrible fall from Rudy when he reared but what was Seb worried about? Yeah, that's right – Sophie."

Even I got a little tired of going on about it but Rosa, it seemed, could listen to me forever. When I started getting ready to leave I gave Meg a goodbye cuddle and, to my delight, was able to put my arms right around Rosa's neck too.

"You're wonderful," I whispered. "Wait till Mom sees you –"

The roan mare's head came up sharply as she turned to look at the gate and there, smiling as she watched us, stood Mom. I lowered my arms slowly and walked over to her accompanied, of course, by Rosa.

"I don't believe it," Mom's eyes were shining. "That can't be the same horse who spent her first few hours here cowering against a stable wall!"

"Yes," I said proudly.

"I was afraid she had a vicious streak when she nearly flattened poor old Chas, but it was pure terror and not aggression. Have you touched her head yet?"

"Not quite, but we're nearly there and she loves being petted everywhere else," I took one of the small buckets of coarse mix and gave it to Meg. "See if Rosa will come to you for her feed."

Mom carefully held out the bucket so the horse could smell it and walked a few steps away. Rosa, however, preferred to stay with me.

"Go on, you silly girl," I pushed her rump gently. "That's a nice, tasty supper over there."

"You'd better bring her here," Mom laughed. "Before Meg finishes hers and nabs this one as well."

As soon as I moved Rosa did too and once both horses had eaten we left them to enjoy another peaceful night. Rosa, as before, watched me until I was completely out of sight and Mom was more than impressed.

"I can hardly believe it! I thought we had months of work ahead of us but you two have made such a connection – well, I'm speechless."

"That's not like you," I said slyly. "Did you manage to find anything to say to Leo and Sophie before you were struck dumb?"

She nudged me jokily with a bucket. "Don't be cheeky. Yes, I had a word with them. The whole Leo/Sophie thing is over – finished – finito!"

CHAPTER SEVEN

"You mean they're leaving? *Both* of them?" I tried to keep the excitement out of my voice.

"I considered it," she said. She wasn't looking at me so didn't see my face fall. "But the two of them are so desperately eager to be here, and they pleaded so eloquently, that I decided to give them another chance."

"So why did you say it's over?"

"They've agreed, *promised* in fact, to avoid one another whenever possible but to be quiet and polite to each other when they do interact. There's obviously a personality clash between the two of them but Barney and I have made it clear it must not interfere with their, or anyone else's, work."

I thought the two warring students had gotten away with their bad behavior very lightly and said so.

"Mm, your granddad's of the same opinion and I think he'd definitely have thrown Leo out, but he's got a soft spot for Sophie."

This was just too much. Even my grumpy old grandfather was giving the blonde girl preferential treatment!

"I'm surprised," I said carefully. "What's so special about her?"

"Well, he only gave her a place on the course as a favor, you know that, but he's impressed by the work she's putting in. The back injury is a nuisance, of course, but Sophie *really* wants to be here. We can see that, and he admires her courage."

I personally thought Sophie should stay home and watch a training DVD but I told myself I was being mean again. Granddad was the best teacher in the world, and if he thought Sophie's riding knowledge could be improved by being here then that's how it had to be. I wasn't at all happy with the situation and decided gloomily that the entire summer vacation was now ruined. Instead of enjoying every day spent riding horses with Seb I'd now be doing my best to keep out of his way.

"Here I am, avoiding Seb so I don't have to hear him going on and on about how great Sophie is, while she and Leo avoid each other so they don't get in a fight. This place is like a minefield!" I told the roan mare early the next morning. "If it weren't for you, Rosa, *I'd* be the one packing my bags and leaving!"

She blew down her nose thoughtfully, those big dark eyes seeming full of sympathy. The morning cuddle with her did me a lot of good and my sessions with Poppy and Rudy were also very satisfying. Poppy was relaxed enough to let me sit on her right away, while Rudy, with no loutish interruptions to distract him, behaved impeccably, not making the slightest attempt at rearing.

"Excellent," Mom beamed. "I think you should take Jazz out with some company today, to make sure he's got the idea of turning every ride into a race out of his head."

"Sure," I said. I loved riding the Thoroughbred over the meadows. "Will you come with us?"

"I can't. I have that youngster to lunge, and then some schooling. See if Seb wants to give Challenger a pipe-opener after his lesson."

My heart sank. "I think Granddad wants him to concentrate on show training for the Cavel Cup."

"Well yes, but he likes the horses to have some fun time too," she said and looked at her watch. "He and Seb will be in the ring with the students. Run over and see what he says."

I really, *really* didn't want to ask Seb to accompany me. I knew I'd find it hard to talk to him; the easy, carefree relationship we'd shared was changed forever, I was sure, since the moment I'd seen him kiss Sophie.

Maybe one of the students could ride out, I thought hopefully. Tina's a good rider, and so is Leo.

Leo, though his in-your-face personality scared me a bit, was probably the strongest choice, I decided as I stood quietly watching the lesson in the indoor ring. Mounted on Sampson he was negotiating the small but tricky jumping course Seb had set up. Granddad, his shaggy eyebrows lowered, was monitoring every move, correcting each tiny fault in position as it happened, making Leo take the big black horse through each bend and twist until he was satisfied. Or nearly.

"Still not perfect," he said brusquely. "And still not good enough for the Cavel Cup, but you *have* improved."

"Gee thanks," Leo muttered, wiping away the sweat trickling down his face.

"Do you want something, Tamzin?" Granddad called across to me and I felt myself stupidly color up as everyone, including Seb, turned to look at me.

"Mom wants Jazz to have company on the meadows," I found myself stuttering slightly. "So would any of the students –"

82

"Seb can go with you," he interrupted. "I just want to see Challenger go around here once and then it'll do him good to go out."

"It would do *me* a bunch of good too," Leo winked at me as he rode past. "Your grand-daddy is a slave driver!"

I ignored him, standing back as the other five students rode their horses out of the ring, followed on foot by Sophie, looking gorgeous in tight jeans and designer top. I really wasn't looking forward to the next hour or so but couldn't help enjoying watching Seb and Challenger go around the jumping course. Perfectly attuned, horse and rider looked almost like one as they soared effortlessly over each fence, their every stride, bend and turn taken with almost poetic fluidity.

"Mm," said Granddad. Even he was impressed. "Good. Very good. If this horse doesn't win the Cavel Cup – well, there's no justice in this world, that's all I can say."

"You don't suppose the Boss thinks I'm doing an OK job, do you?" Seb grinned at me but I felt too uptight and self-conscious to return it.

"Sure he does. Uh – sorry about you having to ride out. Mom wants Jazz to –"

"Have company, yeah you said." He looked at me,

puzzled. "What's the matter, Tamzin? Are you still mad at me for something?"

Oh yeah, all he'd done was either rave about Sophie, or totally ignore me, yet he was surprised I was less than happy to be with him.

"I'm all right," I said grouchily.

"Look, I'm sorry I sounded off about your granddad the other day. He and I – well, we don't always agree, and as usual I thought he was being too harsh."

You mean too harsh on Sophie, I thought sullenly. I shrugged and said aloud, "I don't get involved with students, I just ride horses."

"Yeah, I know, and I also know that when you're old enough to compete in adult competitions it'll be you riding Challenger and not me, but I'm fine with that. I love the teaching side; I just wish the Boss would lighten up sometimes."

Although I did actually agree, I wasn't going to say so, thinking privately that the old man had shown a surprisingly lenient side when it came to Leo and in particular, *of course*, Sophie. It was too complicated to say all that, and if I did Seb would think I was being unfair to Sophie. I figured it was better to let him think I resented him riding in the Cavel Cup so I just gave a grunt, which sounded, even to me, a lot like the sound Granddad makes. On this note of misunderstanding and sulkiness we rode out of the yard in a distinctly chilly mood. Jazz, in complete contrast, was his usual happy self, moving along the lane in a loose, free striding walk.

"He – uh – he looks good," Seb made an effort to break the glum silence between us.

I nodded, trying hard to shift the black cloud I was under. "Yeah, the work we've been putting in, up-hill trotting and so on, has built up some muscle."

"Has he run off with you at all?" Seb asked politely and I wanted to scream, What do you care if he has? It doesn't matter if *I* get hurt, does it?

Instead I shook my head dumbly.

"Oh come on, Tam." He brought Challenger alongside us and looked at me, his blue eyes soft with concern. "I know I was out of line, sounding off about the Boss like that, but this isn't like you. You don't *do* girly sulking! I can't believe you're upset about me riding Challenger, so if I've done something else to upset you, tell me!"

If I'd started I could have given him a list a mile long but of course I didn't. "It's nothing," I mumbled. "I'm totally fine about Challenger and looking forward to watching you two win the Cavel Cup. It's just – I don't like the atmosphere at Highfields much these days. Everyone's fighting."

"You mean that big ape, Leo?" His fingers tightened on the reins, making the big white horse break into a brief jog. "Sorry, Challenger, sorry, boy. Ignore Leo, Tam – he's just too wound up with ambition. He thinks he's got a good chance in the Cavel Cup even though he's seen what Challenger can do."

OK, I thought, let's talk about Leo; it's a safer subject than Sophie. Instead I said, "Leo's ambitious and he does work hard even if he seems pretty hyper all the time."

"You've noticed that? He's always in a rage, never chills out and relaxes, but I guess that's just his over-the-top way. Look what he's like with Sophie!"

Oh, here we go.

"He doesn't like her, you mean?"

"*Like* her? You've heard of love at first sight?"

I looked at him. Was he going to tell me that's what happened between him and Sophie? "You mean –?"

"I mean it's like Leo's been infected with *hate* at first sight! He was on Sophie's case the minute she arrived, shouting at her, insulting her, it was – *unreal*!"

"It's like you said, he's probably too ambitious. He's desperate to be good enough for the Cavel Cup and he resents the attention Sophie gets."

"She doesn't take up that much of Mr. Raynor's time," Seb protested. "She's really quiet, works on her

86

notes, and concentrates hard. The Boss wasn't at all impressed with her at first but Sophie's shown such dedication despite the pain she's in –"

I couldn't stand hearing much more about Saint Sophie.

"Oh," I interrupted. "Did Jazz pick up a stone just now? I think he hobbled for a pace."

"Let me look." In an instant he was on the ground, inspecting the chestnut's feet. "No, he's fine," he said, remounting and turning his gorgeous eyes toward me. "Anyway, let's leave all the egos, and the problems they're creating, back at the yard, Tamzin."

"OK," I said. I couldn't resist his smile. "Enjoy the moment, isn't that what they say?"

"And it's a beautiful moment," he waved a hand at the view. "Look at that."

We'd left the road behind us and were trotting up the springy turf trail leading to the meadows. The lovely countryside spread before and around us, gently undulating in soft green and gold folds to the far distance. Jazz snorted eagerly but I was pleased he didn't shake his head and make a crafty snatch at the bit.

"Good boy," I told him. "My hands can stay this soft when you behave like that, so when I ask for a canter I don't want you plunging into a gallop."

Seb and Challenger stayed beside us as we flowed

into the glorious three-beat stride, moving across the summer grass in perfect symmetry. The sun shone from a lofty sapphire sky, warming the soft breeze that lifted the horses' manes and sent my own glossy dark hair streaming behind me like a banner. Seb was the perfect person to have along when I was riding one of our problem horses, keeping the beautiful gray in sympathetic harmony so that even the most wayward horses gained confidence. Jazz, the headlong, frantic desire for speed forgotten, was filled instead with a calmer joy, every finely tuned muscle reveling in the motion of cantering. We stopped on the crest of the highest slope, sitting quietly as the horses stretched their necks and took deep breaths of crystal-clear air. Seb and I being together like this felt so natural it was hard to stay aloof and, as we walked the horses toward a small wooded area, I found myself laughing and talking with him the way I'd always done.

"Enjoy the moment" seemed a good maxim and it was easy up here in the sunlight to forget the cloud of gloom I'd been wallowing under.

"Does Jazz like to jump?" Seb asked. Now we'd entered the woods and Seb was looking around. "We could build a couple of easy jumps so he can have some fun."

"I've taken him over a few logs," I said. "And he seemed to like it."

Jazz, in fact, absolutely loved jumping, and though he got very excited, he still didn't attempt to bolt in the mindless, frantic way we'd been trying to cure.

"The trick is to give Jazz something other than racing to think about," I said, patting him as he cantered beautifully between the two jumps made from fallen branches. "Now that it's no longer a habit he's having a terrific time doing other things."

Seb was great, dragging branches and logs around to build the inviting jumps and carefully pacing the distances between them to get it just right for the chestnut's long frame.

"He's got the same stride pattern as Challenger," he said, grinning up at me. "It's amazing how well you ride him, considering how big he is and how tiny you –"

"Oh, don't start all that," I said, hoping he wasn't comparing Sophie's long, long legs to mine. "We'll have one more try, and then you and Challenger can show us how it should be done."

It was great, just the two of us and the horses in the cool, dappled shade of the little woods, and I was feeling much better about life as I slid out of the saddle to grab more branches.

"Hang on to Jazz," I said and handed Seb the reins.

"I'd better build these jumps a bit higher or you two won't even notice they're there."

"We're good but we're not *that* good!" Seb joked, and then reached in his pocket as his cell phone beeped.

"Text message from Sophie," he held the phone up and squinted at it.

I turned and started to walk away, feeling the familiar sinking sensation. Sophie. It had to be. Then, with a sudden, explosive squawk, a bird sheltering on a low branch took off, swooping past so close I felt its wing brush my cheek. Jazz, startled and alarmed by the unexpected noise and movement, shied sideways, pulling the reins from Seb's hand. In blind panic the chestnut horse clattered clumsily forward, knocking me to the ground, and as I was falling his sharp hooves gave me a hefty blow. I felt a huge burst of pain inside my left temple, followed by a searing, burning sensation running the length of my leg. For an instant stars, rainbows and fireworks flashed across my eyes and then I felt myself sliding down, down into a black pit of oblivion where there was nothing, nothing at all.

CHAPTER EIGHT

I was very lucky; the bang on my head knocked me out completely for several hours so by the time I woke up the worst of the trauma was over. The first thing I saw when I opened my eyes was my granddad's face, tanned, leathery and somber as usual.

"Hello," I said, a bit weakly – and got the shock of my life when his lower lip trembled and tears welled up in his eyes.

"Tamzin," he reached out and took my hand between his and I could feel his fingers shaking. "You're all right."

"Yeah, course," I moved my head gingerly. "Got a headache, though. And my leg feels funny, all heavy."

"It's broken," Mom stepped forward and smiled down at me, tactfully masking the old man from view as he fumbled with a handkerchief. "Jazz trod on it. It's a simple break, fortunately, but it would have been very painful if you'd been conscious."

"I'm glad I wasn't, then," I said, feeling strangely detached. "Is Jazz OK?"

"Yes, he didn't go far. He just barged into you and then sort of stumbled to a halt in a bush, Seb says."

Seb.

"How did I get here?" I looked vaguely around the hospital. "Seb didn't *carry* me, did he?"

Mom laughed, and though she was being ultra cool I could see huge relief in her eyes. "No, he called an ambulance, and then called us. My first thought was that Jazz had thrown you."

"Nah, he wouldn't do that, and he didn't mean to knock me over, either. He was scared and he panicked."

"Seb feels terrible. He says it was his fault," Mom said and turned to Granddad who'd finished mopping his eyes. "The poor guy's in an awful state about it, isn't he, Barney?"

"So he should be," the old man said, his voice back to normal. "Totally irresponsible, fiddling around with a phone when he's in charge of two horses."

"It was an accident, Granddad." I closed my eyes again.

"We should get the doctor to see her, Kate." There
was a hurried scraping sound as he pushed his chair back.
"He'll need to check to make sure she's completely well."

"OK," Mom agreed. "But I can see that she's fine."

I *was* fine, of course, apart from the fact that my
leg was completely encased in a cast, but the doctor
insisted that I stay in for a couple of days, "under
observation."

"You've had a nasty bump on the head and we like
to monitor things like that very carefully," he told me.

"But I can't stay here," I said, looking at him as if
he was crazy. "I need to see Rosa."

"Maybe she could come in to see you instead," he
suggested kindly and Mom put a hand on mine to calm
me down.

"Rosa's a horse, Doctor. There's no need for Tamzin
to worry, though. Seb has promised to spend every
spare minute he has with her."

Oh sure, I thought, like he'll give Rosa priority over
his precious Sophie! I didn't say anything then, but as
soon as she walked through the door the next day I said,
"How's Rosa? Did she let you near her? Did you –"

"Message from Seb," she handed me a huge bunch
of flowers. "These are for you. He's sorry he can't visit
in person but he's spending the time with Rosa and he
says to tell you she's fine. She ate all her supper last

night and wouldn't let him touch her, but this morning he stroked her shoulder."

"She let me go right up her neck," I said ungratefully.

"Well, in a day or two you can get reacquainted," Mom said and put the flowers in a vase. "You won't be riding for weeks, so you'll have plenty of time to be with her."

The two days in the hospital absolutely dragged, even though as soon as I was allowed out of bed I put in a lot of effort practicing getting around. I was determined not to go home in a wheelchair, so worked hard on my technique with two elbow crutches. Everyone in the ward was nice – don't get me wrong – and they all signed their names and did cute drawings on my cast, but I couldn't *wait* to leave.

"I've bet your granddad I know exactly where you'll head the minute we get home." Mom helped me into the back seat of the car, and my left leg stuck out across it.

"To see Rosa," I said immediately. "How come Granddad didn't visit me again? He seemed really upset to see me hurt, but –"

"Once he knew you were all right he had to concentrate on Highfields." Her smile was a bit sad, I thought. "Seb is working nonstop, what with extra riding on Jazz and Rudy plus all the visits to Rosa, so we're all stretched pretty thin."

"Sorry," I said, "for being a nuisance."

"You're not – and don't go worrying about Granddad. You know what he's like. He's no good at expressing his feelings."

It was great to be home. Mom won her bet, of course – the first place I wanted to go was the smallest paddock. She helped me with the gate and then stood back and watched as I lurched across the grass on my crutches. The two horses were way across the field and Rosa looked up immediately but, unsure who this clumsy figure on two crutches could be, hung back behind Meg. I took a deep breath and stood still.

"Rosa. Come on, baby, it's me."

She pricked her ears forward eagerly and gave a small whicker.

"Good girl, come on," I crooned and to my delight she moved toward me, first at an uncertain walk, then at trot, finally flowing into a superb canter as she recognized me for sure.

I felt, stupidly, big, fat tears of joy roll down my face. I'd been terrified that she'd forget me, worrying that the bond we'd forged had been broken forever, so to see the beautiful horse running so eagerly to greet me was the best tonic in the world.

"Steady now," I spoke quietly. "Whoa, Rosa."

She came to a halt in front of me, bringing her lovely head close to mine as she breathed in my scent. We stood like that for ages, with me leaning on one crutch as my other hand rubbed and stroked and petted the roan mare's neck.

"Wow," Mom said as she came over to join us. "That was one of the most touching things I've ever seen. She was overjoyed to see you. Overjoyed. It's amazing!"

"Mm," I managed to say, choked with emotion myself. "It's just as well, since I'll be spending most of my day with her from now on."

"Yeah? You'll get bored, won't you?"

"Well, I'll miss riding but at least I can help Rosa get over her old fear, so that's work worth doing," I said, still trying to pretend she was just another project. "What about Poppy and the others?"

"I'm riding Poppy. I'm not much bigger than you so that's OK. Seb's riding Jazz and Rudy – he says he's going to give up his day off until you're better."

I felt a mean glow that he wouldn't have much time left for Sophie but stamped on it hard.

"I don't know why he's taking all the blame. It was just one of those freaky things, a total accident."

"He says he wasn't concentrating, that he was reading

98

a text message." Mom looked at me. "It was from Sophie, apparently."

"Yeah?" I thought I sounded cool and indifferent.

"Mm, she's interested in him, I think."

"Oh?" I was not quite so cool. "How about her and Leo? Are they still fighting?"

"Leo mutters and moans about her but he keeps out of her way pretty much."

"Good," I smiled as Rosa lifted her nose and ruffled my hair. "I'll stay here for a while if you need to get back to work."

"Are you sure?" She looked doubtful. "Shall I bring the wheelchair in here? You might get tired and –"

"I'm not using it," I said firmly. "The more I walk on crutches the stronger I'll get. Rosa's already getting used to them, look."

"Oh well, *she's* the most important consideration, obviously," Mom laughed as she walked back to the gate. "Phone me if you want anything."

"OK," I checked to make sure I had my cell phone. "See you at dinnertime."

One day when I've got a calculator handy I'm going to work out exactly how many hours I spent with Rosa teaching her not to be head-shy. I know it was a *lot*; everyone said so, including Seb.

"At least I always know where to find you

nowadays," he joked as he climbed over the gate the following evening.

"Well, I can't go far, can I?" I made a face at the heavy cast and his face fell.

"Tam, I'm so sorry –"

"Oh, give it a rest!" I pretended to hit him with one of my crutches and changed the subject to my favorite topic. "So, how do you think Rosa's doing?"

"Fantastic. I saw her being unloaded from the truck that first day and I honestly hardly recognize her as the same horse. She was petrified, sweating and cowering away from anyone, and look at her now!"

Rosa, her eyes closed with bliss, was reveling in my touch, not even blinking when my fingers moved from the top of her neck to her head.

"Mom says she's nearly ready to have a head collar put on she can be tried in a stable again," I said, and then changed to a baby talk crooning. "But we're not going to rush things now, are we, my beautiful Rosa?"

"I guess there's no point," Seb agreed. "The rest of us have enough on our hands in the yard with you not being able to ride. Rosa might just as well enjoy an extended vacation with Meg while you keep working your magic on her."

"I think so too." It was like the old days, I thought, the nice time before Sophie when Seb and I had been best friends. "But I don't know about magic. Rosa's trust is being restored, that's all. I guess she'll let just about anyone near her now."

"Don't you believe it," he shook his head. "Sophie tagged along last night but I had to ask her to leave because Rosa wouldn't even come near us for her feed."

"Yeah?" I stared at him.

"It wasn't until Sophie had gone that Rosa let me approach her."

"I wonder why? You don't think the groom who beat her looked like Sophie, do you?" I was half-kidding but he replied totally seriously.

"I think it's the voice. Rosa loves listening to you but as soon as she heard Sophie she backed off right away."

I'd always found Sophie's high-pitched, slightly whining tone immensely irritating but didn't say so.

"Mom says Rosa lets you stroke her shoulder," I said, deciding it safer to stay away from discussing Sophie. "I wonder if she'll accept you doing it near her head?"

Seb, as I knew he would be, was incredibly patient, moving his hand gently up the roan mare's neck, taking his time to reassure her with his voice and calm, unthreatening actions.

"Have you ridden Jazz today?" I asked, leaning a bit wearily on my crutches.

"Yeah, the Boss rode with me and he got Tina and Kay to come along on the way back. I did exactly the same as you, copied your technique, in fact, and Jazz didn't snatch at the bit or try to bolt off even when we all cantered up a hill."

"Great – that's one boy who'll be going home soon," I said, genuinely pleased for the chestnut horse and his owner. "How about Rudy?"

He made a face. "Not so good. I wasn't quick enough and he managed to put in a half-rear, but I think he was just testing it out."

"It's become a habit. We've just got to persevere till we've taught him to forget all about it," I said and couldn't help sighing. "Six weeks without riding! I can't imagine it – I'll go nuts!"

"Mm, spending hours tickling Rosa's ears is rewarding, I know, but it's pretty dull stuff compared with what you've been used to." His blue eyes were full of concern. "Tam, I'm really –"

"If you say sorry again I really will use these crutches on you!" I threatened.

Rosa's eyes opened wide and her head came up sharply, but it wasn't me who'd startled her.

"Seb! Seb!" The high-pitched twang was

unmistakable and I felt my shoulders sag as Seb turned to look over at the gate.

"Hi, Sophie."

"You couldn't be an absolute darling, I suppose?" Her teeth gleamed even from a distance. "Mr. Raynor's given us all evening chores and mine's the tack room but the saddles are too heavy."

"She can't lift anything," Seb muttered. "Her back's still really bad."

"You'd better go and help her, then," I said and gave a tight smile.

"What about you?"

"I'm with Rosa," I said brightly, "so I'm fine."

I tried not to watch him walk away and turned my back completely when he reached the gate in case he kissed Sophie again. There was an old tree trunk nearby where a giant oak had fallen years ago and I was pleased to find it made a reasonable seat, allowing me to stretch out the cumbersome cast quite comfortably in front of me. Rosa obligingly stayed close, contentedly grazing, and we were still together when Mom brought the evening buckets of feed. I had my usual cuddle with Meg, demonstrated the ease with which I could now stroke Rosa's head, and finally limped off to the house, feeling as tired as if I'd been riding all day.

That session more or less set the pattern for the next few weeks. I found myself totally in everyone's way in the yard, taking so long to hobble through even the simplest of chores that it was easier if I just stayed away, so apart from sleeping and eating, I spent practically the whole time in the tucked-away paddock with Rosa and Meg. Our relationship blossomed, and with everyone being very good about visiting us whenever they could Rosa gradually became confident with other people too. She would now calmly accept having a head collar fitted, but although Mom talked about leading her back to the yard to make sure she was also OK in a stable she just didn't have time to do it.

"I didn't realize how much work you do, Tamzin," she remarked and ruffled my hair affectionately. "We're really missing your input, you know!"

"Glad to hear it," I said. I was hobbling faster but still hobbling, obviously. "Why don't we leave Rosa's stable training until I've gotten this cast off?"

"Mm," she said and looked at me. "You wouldn't be wanting to delay things? I know you don't want her to go but that's the object of all this, Tam. Rosa *has* to go home."

"I know that." I lay awake crying about it most nights. "But there's no hurry. You told her owners re-schooling would probably take a long time and need a lot of patience."

"True, and I will say you've done a fabulous job. I can't believe the things that once-terrified horse will let you do now."

I smiled, hugging to myself a secret only Rosa, Meg and I knew. Not only did the roan mare accept my every touch, not only did she still follow my every (limping) move like a devoted puppy – she'd also allowed me to *ride* her – not once but several times!

CHAPTER NINE

The first time was almost by accident. I know that
sounds crazy but it's totally true. I'm very aware, with
the job I do, that safety comes first, so given that Rosa
wasn't even wearing a head collar, let alone a bridle,
and I had only one leg that worked, there's no way I'd
have planned it. Granddad had mentioned that no one
had checked any of the paddocks fencing recently and I
thought I could help in a small way by making sure the
field was OK. It's not a long or difficult task normally,
and it can even be pleasant, walking around the
perimeter of the pretty paddock and making sure each
post and rail is secure, but, like everything else, with
one leg in a cast it was a prolonged and tiring struggle.
Using the elbow crutches I'd managed to reach the
furthest line, accompanied of course by my faithful

Rosa, and was practically on my knees (or knee in my case!) with fatigue. There was no handy tree trunk to sit on over there and if I flopped down on the grass I couldn't get up again, so I sort of draped myself against the fence itself. By standing on the lower rung with my good right foot and hauling with my arms I managed an ungainly, crab-like ascent to sit on the top bar. The only trouble was that the weight of my left leg in its cast kept dragging down uncomfortably.

"If you stand just there, Rosa," I told her. "I could rest my broken leg across your back, then I wouldn't have to support it like this."

As if she'd understood every word (and I honestly think she did) the roan mare positioned herself beside me, calmly allowing me to drape the injured leg across her withers. From there, of course, it was just a slide and a little wriggle until I was sitting astride her, and the sheer bliss of our togetherness brought a great lump of emotion to my throat. I croaked, "Walk on, Rosa," and she did, carrying me carefully along the whole line of fencing. I could use my right leg for gentle direction aids and Rosa seemed to understand she must ignore the dead weight of the cast on her near side. I've ridden some wonderful horses over the years, in dressage, show jumping and schooling, and enjoyed exhilarating gallops with them across the stunning meadows, but nothing,

nothing has ever thrilled me as much as that first time Rosa took me around the small, secluded paddock.

It was a heady, glorious feeling – and one I couldn't resist repeating. I didn't dare tell Mom or Granddad, of course, but every day after that Rosa and I enjoyed a ride around. I was careful to choose a time when I knew everyone was busy with schooling and training and I knew Rosa's sensitive ears would flicker if she heard anyone approaching. Most of the students were very good about taking time at the end of their busy schedule to visit Rosa, and every day she gained more confidence. Seb was right about her disliking certain voices. Rosa still put her ears back when she heard Sophie though she now allowed the blonde girl to touch her. Having a pretty low opinion of Sophie myself, I thought Rosa's reluctance to accept her showed good taste, but was a bit upset that the roan mare also took a while to take to Chas.

"Chas has a voice like a cement mixer filled with gravel," Seb laughed when I told him. "Did she let him touch her head, though?"

"Oh yeah, she's not shying away from anyone now," I said proudly. "And I'm sure she'll be OK when her vacation's over and we try her out in a stable."

"You're saving that till after your cast comes off, right?" Seb gave me his gorgeous, if slightly tired, smile.

"Yep, only a week to go – and that's when this student course finishes too, isn't it?"

"Yeah, but there's only a short gap until the start of the next one," he pulled Rosa's ears gently.

I wondered if he was sad at the thought of Sophie leaving so said in a very upbeat tone, "Just long enough for you and Challenger to win the Cavel Cup."

"Don't let Leo hear you say that! He still says he and Sampson are going to take it."

"No way!" I said bluntly. "You're in a different league altogether."

"Thanks, Tam, but that's Challenger, not me. And the Boss, of course. I still argue with the old man every so often, but I've got nothing but respect for him – he's a fantastic teacher."

"Yeah, he is, but even he can't work miracles. I heard him say Leo has the talent but not the temperament."

"Yeah, Leo's still a pain," Seb agreed. "Though he's kept his word and left Sophie alone. She still bugs him, though; you can tell by the way he looks at her."

"Oh?" I couldn't tell from his voice whether he and the blonde girl were still an item or not. "Maybe he's still annoyed that she attends all the lessons. She works hard at her notes, Granddad says, but she'll find it hard to put them in practice at first. Studying theory's good but it only takes a few weeks off riding for your muscles turn to mush. Mine have gone all soft and soggy."

"All this time without sitting on a horse! It must have been torture for you."

"Mm," I didn't meet his eye. "Except it's given me plenty of time to help Rosa. I think her fear of being handled, and certainly her head-shy habit, is completely cured."

"Terrific," he patted her. "Oh Tam, did you know we had a call from Jazz's owner? She's thrilled at the way he's behaving now, and soon Rosa will be back with her owners and they'll be telling you the same thing – Tamzin, are you all right?"

Huge, fat tears had welled up in my eyes, spilling down my cheeks before I could stop them. I moved clumsily, trying to hide my face, "I – I –"

"Oh, Tam," he said softly. "You really love this horse, don't you?"

"Yes," I looked up defiantly, not caring if my nose was red and my face all blotchy. "Yeah, I do, but you're not to tell my mom or my granddad, do you hear me?"

"But maybe they could –"

"No, they couldn't," I leaned against Rosa's neck and buried my face in her beautiful mane. "This is

what we do. This is what Highfields is for – mending *other people's* horses. Rosa belongs to someone else and I've always known that."

"Tamzin, I'm really sorry," he said and put a hand hesitantly on my shoulder. "You've had a rotten summer –"

"No, I haven't." I sniffed unbeautifully. "It's been great being with Rosa."

His words had hit home though, and I spent a sleepless night, tossing and turning at the thought of waking up one morning knowing Rosa was gone. I didn't say anything at breakfast, of course, but just listened to Mom planning out the day ahead.

"Everyone's at the farrier's lecture today," she told Granddad. "So it's an ideal time for us to school Challenger."

"Good idea; we can use the ring." Granddad enjoys working with Mom and comparing notes on a horse's progress. "Seb is perfectly capable of helping with the demonstration and it'll be good for him to take on the full responsibility of looking after the students."

"That's settled then – oh, would you like to watch how we get on, Tamzin?"

I didn't want to waste one minute of my remaining days with Rosa on anything but her, so I shook my head.

"No thanks, I – uh – want to try something with

Rosa," I grabbed my crutches and hobbled off before either of them could start on the, "Don't get too fond of that horse," lecture, and spent the first twenty minutes bawling into patient Rosa's neck.

It was another beautiful summer day and a great shame to waste it being miserable, so I managed to cheer up enough to enjoy our daily ride around the field. As usual the roan mare looked after me carefully, never ever shying or being skittish, and standing beautifully while I clambered aboard. She then stepped out lightly with a lovely, even pace to ensure I didn't get jolted. The grass was thick, nibbled short by the two horses, but still lush, and Rosa's neat hooves made little sound. At the far end we turned smoothly and began walking the long line of fencing bordered on its other side by a small, dense wooded area. Wrapped in my favorite daydream where Rosa and I live happily ever after, I didn't hear the voices at first, but then as they became louder and angrier I put my hand on the roan pony's neck, asking her to halt.

"Leo!" It was Sophie, of course, sounding shrill and petulant. "I can't take any more of this!"

"*You* can't?" Leo's voice was rough and angry, "What do you think it's been like for me these last few weeks?"

"There was no need for you to walk out of the lecture like that. I only stood next to you because –"

"Because you wanted to drive me crazy! Go back to the ring, Sophie; take your stupid textbook and your stupid folder and leave me alone."

"Don't worry, I'm going!"

They were getting nearer now, only just behind the trees on the other side of the fence, and for a panicky moment I couldn't think what to do. I didn't dare keep riding; if they saw me and told Mom she'd be furious and would certainly ban me from riding Rosa, maybe even from seeing her altogether.

Dismounting was easy, if not stylish, with Rosa standing as steady as a rock while I lowered myself to the ground, balancing on my good leg and holding onto her mane for support. I'd just straightened up and gotten back on my crutches when she turned her intelligent head toward the fence.

Sophie, her face flushed, came storming out of the woods, marching straight for the field. Thrusting the pink folder under one arm, she scrambled nimbly onto the top bar of the fence.

"Just stay there and sulk, loser!" She twisted around as she yelled at Leo, then slid to the grass almost alongside Rosa and me. "I'm going to give Seb a big kiss to say sorry – oh, and I'll tell Mr. Raynor you couldn't be bothered to finish the course, shall I?"

With a roar of frustration Leo crashed through a

clump of bramble and ran at the fence, scaling it in one athletic surge.

I saw Rosa's ears go back and she sidestepped nervously.

"Come on, you two," I said, sounding like an elderly aunt or something. "Act your age and stop fighting."

"Oh no, if Prom Queen Sophie wants a fight she can have one," Leo took a step toward the three of us.

Despite him being big and pretty tough-looking, I wasn't scared, being sure there was no way he'd physically hurt either of us, but I wasn't prepared for Sophie's reaction. She screamed loudly, making Rosa start nervously, and even Meg looked up from her grazing way across the field.

"Stop playacting!" Leo roared, and to my amazement she flew at him, long golden hair streaming behind her, long varnished nails stretched out in front.

I think he tried to sidestep, making a lunging movement to avoid her, but it sent him crashing heavily against the fence. I clearly heard the sound of cracking, splintering wood and then, shockingly, he was on the ground, clutching at his leg as a great crimson stain spread rapidly above his right knee. Sophie, at a decibel level you wouldn't believe, *really* started screaming then, dropping her folder in agitation as she bent to look at him.

"Call a doctor – get an ambulance – oh, no, look at the blood!"

I fumbled in my pocket, my fingers scrambling.

"Tamzin," Leo, his face contorted with pain, put out a hand. "Catch her, Tamzin – she's fainting."

Sophie had gone the color of chalk and, as I turned to look, her knees buckled and she crumpled limply to the ground. With shaking hands I dialed 911 and babbled our address.

"Put a compress on the wounded leg," said the authoritative voice on the other end of the phone line. "A handkerchief will do, any piece of folded cloth to stem the flow of blood. And make sure the airways are clear on the girl who's blacked out."

It was difficult, moving clumsily on my crutches, but somehow I managed. Rosa was wonderful, staying close enough for me to lean on her while I, not having a tissue, frantically tore the sleeve off my shirt.

"Press hard on the injury," I passed on the instructions to Leo, who was now even whiter than the frighteningly still blonde girl. "I need to make sure Sophie's breathing properly."

Again I was grateful for Rosa's physical support and her comforting presence as I awkwardly bent to check the unconscious figure. Sophie was stirring a little as she started to come around, but it took several more

minutes before she could sit up. Leo, by then, was slumped with eyes closed and Sophie let out a moan when she looked across at him.

"He's all right," I said sharply, desperate to keep her from fainting again. "The wound isn't bleeding so much, but that cloth needs pressure on it. Put your hand over his to make sure it stays in place."

As though moving in a trance she did as I said, but although a faint color was returning to her face she still looked deeply shocked. Rosa gave a small whicker, turning her head toward the gate and a moment later I saw, to my enormous relief, an ambulance approaching it. Someone was running ahead to open the gate and I waved my arms above my head.

"Over here – we're over here!"

The ambulance bucketed swiftly toward us and within minutes two calm, capable paramedics were tending to both Leo and Sophie.

"Leave me," the blonde girl said, her voice now a whisper. "It's my – it's Leo who needs to be looked after."

Mom ran up, panting, throwing her arms around me, and as I cuddled her I felt the gentle touch of Rosa's soft nose on the back of my neck.

"She's giving you a kiss too," Mom said, half laughing, half crying. "Oh Tamzin, when we saw the ambulance heading this way we thought it was *you* who was injured."

"No, I'm fine," I said. I lifted my head and watched as Leo was efficiently put on a stretcher and placed into the ambulance while Sophie, wrapped in a thermal blanket, stumbled behind.

"Are you all right?" Mom released me and spoke gently to her. "You're going to the hospital to get checked over?"

"It was my fault. All my fault." Tears rolled down Sophie's still pale face, her nose was streaming and her skin blotchy.

"It was an accident," I shuffled forward on my crutches but, zombie-like, she walked up the steps into the back of the ambulance.

The driver set off immediately, leaving Mom and me to follow slowly across the field.

"It's just as well that Rosa and Meg aren't the escaping type," Mom tried to joke. "I left the gate wide open, look."

"Meg wouldn't bother and Rosa, well, she just wants to stay with me. She was terrific, Mom. She didn't even take off when Sophie started screaming, and you know how she hates loud voices."

"What was the girl screaming about? All the blood, I suppose."

"No, she passed out when she saw that. She and Leo were having a fight, and when she said she'd tell Granddad Leo came after her. She screamed her head off and kind of flew at him."

"They've been at each other's throats since day one," Mom shook her head. "I've never understood it. Tam, when you said she went for him what do you mean? She didn't do that to his leg, surely?"

"No, it was a complete accident. He tried to dodge her and barged into the fence. One of the slats broke and pierced his leg."

"Dreadful," she shuddered. "And with Sophie being phobic about the sight of blood it was lucky you were there. Oh, look, there's your granddad. He's probably been in a terrible state; he'll be *so* relieved to see you."

I thought that was probably an exaggeration but, to my surprise, as Granddad got close I could see his hands were shaking and his voice was emotional.

"Tamzin, you're all right, you're all right! I tried to stop the ambulance to find out what happened but they were in a tearing hurry to get to the hospital. I thought – I thought you were inside, seriously injured."

"Barney, she's fine," Mom took his old hands between hers. "Leo's been badly hurt but Tamzin is *fine*."

"I – I managed to put Challenger away," he said,

obviously deeply shaken. "But I left the yard a real mess, students' horses everywhere and –"

"I'll go and help Seb sort it out," Mom patted his hand gently before she released it. "You and Tam go back to the house and have a hot drink. You've both had a bad shock."

Granddad nodded and I could see that his bottom lip was trembling. I wanted to give him a cuddle or at least hold his hand but the cumbersome crutches prevented me from doing either.

"Don't be upset, Granddad," I gave him my best, most loving smile.

"Oh, Tamzin," his voice, normally a powerful boom, was still shaky, "I want to tell you something."

"Later, Granddad," I hobbled as close to him as I could. "Mom's right, you've had a shock."

"No, I need to tell you now. Seeing that ambulance, thinking it was for you, brought everything back and – well I didn't tell you at the time but I should have. When I saw you in the hospital a few weeks ago, when I saw you lying so still, so pale," he swallowed. "I felt the same as I did when I lost Carl. Your dad was everything to me and yet, do you know, Tamzin, I never told him? Not once did I ever tell my son I loved him."

Tears welled up in my eyes and I couldn't speak.

"I should have said it to him and to you too, but

I'm a stubborn old man and I find it hard to say things like that."

"It's all right, Granddad," I felt the tears spilling over. "I know you love me, just like my dad knew."

Silently, he put his hand on my shoulder and when we got to the gate I leaned my crutches against it and we wrapped our arms right around each other in a long, emotional hug.

CHAPTER TEN

Rosa, still firmly at my side, finally broke us up by nibbling gently at my hair.

"Don't tell me you're jealous, young lady!" Granddad patted her, turning his head away as he tried to get his emotions back under control. "Tamzin doesn't have to keep all her hugs just for you!"

"She does seem to think I should," I was glad to help lighten the atmosphere. "I can't think why – just because I spend every waking minute with her!"

We petted both horses for a while until I could see Granddad had stopped shaking and was back to his usual, strong, practical self.

He didn't ask any questions about Leo's accident until we'd returned to the house and were drinking hot chocolate.

"I don't understand why they were there," he said, his bushy eyebrows drawn together in a frown. "*All* the students should have been at the farrier's lecture in the ring with Seb."

"He and Sophie argued," I said. "Leo left the lecture to get away from her but she followed."

"Where was Seb while all this was going on? He was supposed to be in charge."

"I was helping the farrier with his demonstration," Seb walked into the kitchen. "I saw Sophie leave but one of the horses was acting up and I couldn't go after her."

"Didn't you realize Leo was missing too?" Granddad glared at him.

"Not until a while later. I went outside to look for both of them but neither was around."

"So that was that? You went back into the ring despite the fact you *knew* Leo was a threat to Sophie?"

"It wasn't like that! I couldn't just abandon the rest of the students to round up a couple of hotheads," Seb had gone pale.

"The description certainly fits Leo, whose temperament has always been suspect, but Sophie is a quiet, vulnerable girl," Granddad's eyes were flashing. "You should at least have told me they'd both disappeared."

"I didn't even know they were together." Poor Seb

was as startled by his telling-off as I was. "Leo's never very interested in attending lectures and I assumed he'd lost interest."

"Whereas in fact he was making one of his vitriolic attacks on Sophie." Granddad was obviously picturing the girl as a helpless victim.

"Hold on," I put in quickly. "It was Sophie who followed Leo, I told you. He was only trying to get away from her."

"But you saw him scale the fence and come running toward her," Granddad objected.

"Only because she goaded him – she threatened to tell you he'd deliberately cut the lecture and –"

"It's all right, Tam," Seb said quietly. "Whatever I do in this case your Grandfather thinks it's wrong. When I tried to stop Leo from tormenting Sophie I got told off, and now when I kept out of it –"

"Don't try to wriggle out of this," Granddad slammed his hand on the table. "The safety of our students was *your* responsibility and you failed dismally."

"Oh?" A glint of rage gleamed in Seb's eyes. "In which case there's no point in me staying, is there? If you think I'm no good at my job –"

"On this occasion I most certainly do," Granddad was angry too but he spoke with an icy calm. "You let poor little Sophie down and it could be her lying seriously hurt in the hospital. Only sheer chance caused Leo's temper to backfire on him."

"Poor little Sophie!" Seb shouted furiously. "She's not some sweet innocent schoolgirl – she's manipulative – she's –"

"That's enough, Seb," Granddad said, his voice, in contrast, still quiet. "If you can't find any better way of defending your actions than by stooping to a fictitious character assassination I think you should leave."

"Leave? Yeah, right, I'll leave," he turned on his heel. "And don't think you're firing me, *Mr.* Raynor – I quit!"

As he walked out I felt stunned, stymied. "You just meant leave the room – you didn't mean you were firing him, did you, Granddad?"

"You heard Seb," he said, taking a sip of his drink. "I didn't fire him – he resigned."

"He didn't mean it," I said desperately. "He was mad because he thought you were being unfair."

"I don't wish to discuss it," he put down his cup abruptly. "I'm going to call the hospital."

He was just putting the phone down when Mom came in.

"What's going on?" She looked worried. "I just saw Seb stamping out of the yard."

"He's probably gone back to the cottage to pack his things," Granddad spoke quite matter-of-factly. "I've spoken to the hospital. Leo lost quite a lot of blood, but the leg is fixable and Sophie's all right too. She's staying with him, apparently, which I think in the circumstances is very noble of her."

"Noble!" It was my turn to be angry with him. "It was her fault! Yeah all right, it was an accident, but *she* caused it."

"You're overwrought, Tamzin," Granddad said coldly. "I suggest you cool off before you say something you'll regret."

"*You* should be the one doing the regretting," I burst into childish tears. "Chasing Seb away when he did nothing wrong! Now I'm going to lose him as well as Rosa! It's – it's –"

It was, in fact, too much. I couldn't speak, I needed to get away, I needed solace, comfort – I needed Rosa. I could hear Mom questioning Granddad as I hobbled away and part of me wanted her to hear my version of what had happened but I was just too upset. I looked across at the little cottage where Seb stayed and pictured him angrily throwing his belongings in a bag. He had no car, and he'd be trying to catch the bus, which left the nearby village on the hour, and then he'd be gone, out of my life forever.

The thought of Highfields without him, without his wonderful riding skills and his endless patience with the horses, was harder to bear than any personal loss. I thought of calling him, of course, of trying to persuade him to wait till he'd cooled down, to reconsider the decision he'd made in anger, but I knew there was no point. Seb had been deeply hurt and had lost his faith in Granddad's judgment, so only an apology from the old man himself would make him change his mind about leaving.

Rosa had heard my approach and was waiting for me at the gate, looking perfectly calm after the noise and trauma of the morning. I clung to her, sobbing into her neck while I told her about Seb, until gradually I raised my head and looked around me. Tire tracks, where the ambulance had driven into the field, showed in a patch of mud but otherwise it was the usual peaceful scene, with Meg grazing unconcernedly over near the woods. I shuddered at the memory of what had happened there, and as I turned to block out the sight I noticed something shifting and fluttering behind the old horse.

"I'd better check it out," I said, removing my arms from around Rosa's neck and getting back on my crutches.

Together we moved across the grass and as we got

closer to the trees I could make out what had caught my eye. Sophie's folder, its contents strewn over a wide area, lay on the ground, the light breeze catching and lifting the scattered papers. Rosa bent her neck and sniffed curiously at the sheets of paper and I picked up one and looked at it.

"The importance of balance for both horse and rider," I read. "One of Granddad's lessons, Sophie's copied down every word. I suppose we'd better pick them all up, Rosa baby. They're making a pretty awful mess."

The roan mare came with me as I started retrieving all the notes, watching solemnly as I pushed each one back in the folder. Picking up one closely written sheet I was surprised to see an envelope of photographs under it, some of which were also spilling out. My surprise turned to amazement when I realized I was looking at a picture of Sophie and Leo taken against a backdrop of palm trees on an exotic beach. I removed the other pictures and stared down at them.

"Look, Rosa, look at this!"

She rested her soft lips against my cheek and blew gently as if, like me, she couldn't believe what we'd found. The photos covered several months of togetherness, Leo and Sophie on a beach vacation, sitting in a country garden, at a party – even one at a horse show with Leo seated on Sampson while a sulky looking Sophie stood beside the black horse's head.

"They're – they're an item!" I leaned back against Rosa's warm shoulder. "No wonder all their fighting seemed so over the top; they weren't strangers at all."

It was starting to make sense, Sophie's outrageous flirting when Leo was around, her constant attempts to get his attention.

"They've clearly got a history, but something must have happened to make Leo so furious at seeing her here," I told Rosa. "She must have followed him and when he wouldn't have anything to do with her she tried everything to get his attention."

I pictured again the look in Leo's eyes just before he fell. "Including driving him crazy with jealousy! It wasn't Sophie's comment about telling Granddad that made him angry – it was Sophie tormenting him by saying she was going to kiss Seb!"

Rosa nudged my arm in vigorous agreement.

"Seb was right to say she's manipulative; she's been playing us all off against each other ever since she got here. Wait till I show Granddad these photos – he'll realize what she's really like and make that apology to Seb."

I dialed Granddad's number but it was Mom who answered.

"He's not here, Tam," she sounded upset. "I told him it was a bad decision to let Seb go and he's gone off to the lower field on his own. He says he's inspecting the fences but he left his phone so we couldn't bother him – he's pretty distressed deep down."

"So he should be," I said with feeling. "He's got the whole thing completely wrong. Sophie was never the victim. Seb was right about her. She's the cause of all this and Granddad shouldn't have blamed Seb."

"Then Granddad must put it right," Mom said. "I'll go and tell him after I've finished with the students."

"That will be too late," I was practically shrieking. "Seb will have left by then – oh, never mind, you can't help it."

Rosa, obviously worried by my agitation, pushed her nose against me.

"You're right," I said, as if she'd spoken. "It's up to you and me. Come on, baby!"

The wonderful horse responded immediately, standing near the fence so I could use it to climb onto her back. I avoided going near the broken, jagged piece of wood that had pierced Leo's leg, and was soon aboard the roan mare. She walked me back to the gate but when I checked my watch I knew we'd have to increase the pace. Bending to shut it behind us I whispered in her ear, "We'll try trotting,

Rosa, and I'll do my best not to bounce around and hurt you."

She set off immediately but the two-time action jolted the heavy cast so much that we were both uncomfortable. Using my right leg I asked for canter and as soon as she flowed into the smooth, even pace I was able to sit into its rhythm. We flew across the grass with me managing to steer using only my one good leg and gentle pressure of my hands. I was holding onto her mane, but by sliding my hand up or down her neck I found Rosa responded beautifully, changing direction as we passed the back of the yard and headed for the lower field in the distance. One of the students spotted us as we passed and called out excitedly. I was aware of a babble of voices behind us and managed a smile to myself. We must, I realized, be quite a sight; the stunning horse, her mane and tail flowing, cantering freely, wearing neither saddle nor bridle while her rider sat lightly – apart from the cumbersome weight of a full cast on her left leg!

The lower field was being rested and was empty of horses so Granddad had left its gate open. This meant I could ask Rosa to canter on, sweeping her way across the grass toward the tall, straight figure at the far side. Granddad turned around to face us when he

heard our approach – and his mouth dropped open with amazement.

"Tamzin! What on earth – why are you –?"

I dropped both hands on the roan mare's neck to bring her to a quiet halt, then fished in my pocket and handed one of the photographs to him.

"Seb was right. Sophie's been lying to us all from the start."

Still dumbstruck by our dramatic appearance, he gazed at the picture for a long time and then he sighed.

"I see. I think I'd better go straight to see Seb – and just hope that he'll let me say I'm sorry."

"OK," I said.

It was a few hours later and Seb and I were in Rosa's field, lolling comfortably on the grass. "How come you knew Sophie wasn't what she seemed even before I found the photos? And why didn't you tell Granddad or Mom, or most of all – ME?"

"I didn't know enough to tell them and *you* didn't seem to like me very much," he said, giving me his gorgeous grin. "Not that I blame you for that. I've been a complete dork. I was sort of – dazzled by Sophie."

"You were a nightmare," I agreed cheerfully. "But I didn't know you'd stopped feeling *that* way about her."

"Well, yeah. For a start she only ever flirted with

me when there was someone around, and it didn't take a genius to work out that she was only doing it to fire Leo up."

"Did you realize they were – or at least had been – together?"

"I thought there must be something in their past but I couldn't work out why they didn't say so."

"Sophie told my Mom everything when she went to the hospital. Apparently for once she's truly devastated. This trauma her dad told us she'd suffered was the breakup of her relationship with Leo. She cheated on him and he dumped her, told her he never wanted to see her again. She wanted him back so she followed him here."

"Why didn't he tell us he knew her?"

"To make her mad. He was still furious and was getting her back. Their relationship was always rocky and they don't seem to care who got caught in the crossfire, Mom says."

"Sophie made a real fool out of me," Seb said ruefully. "Had me running around, doing all her chores because of her bad back – which I'm guessing was pure fiction as well?"

"Oh, yes. She invented that partly to get out of riding. She's hopeless, apparently – and partly in the hope of getting Leo's sympathy. Instead she got

Granddad's – she was always careful to play the quiet, sweet little studious girl when he was around."

"She's a good actress." Seb didn't sound *too* broken hearted, I was glad to hear. "I just hope she's had a bad enough scare to make her behave better in the future."

"She's persuaded Leo to take her back," I said. "She really did pass out when she saw he was hurt, and *he* really was concerned about her. To be honest, I'd say they deserve each other."

"Oh well," Seb said, gently rubbing Rosa's ears as she bent to say hello. "I'll stick to horses, I think. They're a lot more honest. I'm really glad your granddad asked me to stay on at Highfields, Tam."

"He prides himself on being able to judge people, so the fact that Sophie fooled him completely came as quite a shock, and he was truly sorry he'd been so unfair to you."

"Speaking of shocks – what about your poor mother? She told me she'd never get over seeing you and Rosa galloping past the yard."

"We were only cantering," I objected.

"Yeah, and the fact that you had no saddle or bridle and only one working leg doesn't factor into it, I guess? You and this horse are *un*believable!"

I laughed as Rosa blew thoughtfully into his ear, and

as usual I tried not to think about the time it would no longer be "Rosa and me."

It was great having Seb back as my best friend, though, and I was determined to enjoy the short time I had left with Rosa. A week later my leg was out of the cast and the students finished their course. And a few days after that the three of us Raynors were there to cheer on Seb as Challenger won the Cavel Cup in amazing style. It was a wonderful day and I did my best to enjoy the thrill of it all and share the feeling of triumph with Granddad, Mom and Seb. For me, though, every pleasure was bittersweet, tainted by the knowledge that Rosa, my adored Rosa, would soon be leaving. She was perfect; completely cured of the head-shy habit, she allowed any of us to pet and stroke her head and put on a halter or bridle. The terrified horse that had pinned Chas against a stable wall now behaved like a well-schooled, well-mannered – well – angel, I'd guess you'd say.

There really was nothing else we could do to improve her and soon the black, dreadful morning arrived when I knew Mom would phone Rosa's owners and tell them their horse could go home. I hadn't slept, of course, and when I went downstairs I couldn't speak and definitely couldn't eat any

breakfast. I was supposed to be slowly building up
the muscles in my left leg but that morning I ran, ran
with tears already blinding me, straight to Rosa. She
was still lying down with her dear friend, Meg, but
she looked up at once and gave the delighted whinny
of greeting I loved to hear. I kept running, dropping
to my knees to hug her, curling my body against
hers as she lay there. She curved her neck around me
protectively, not minding that my tears were soaking
her warm skin. We lay there, cuddled together, while I
talked to her as always, but this time her calm, loving
presence couldn't stop my crying. An hour later
when we both heard the rattle of the gate that told us
someone was approaching, I was still sniffing and
hiccupping into her now soggy mane.

"It'll be Mom," I said and screwed my eyes tight
shut. "She's come to tell us we have to say goodbye."

"I've only ever seen one other horse lie beside
someone like that," it was Granddad's voice, "and that
was Meg. You and Carl used to take a nap together,
didn't you, Meggie?"

I tried to dry my tears as Rosa and I scrambled to
our feet.

"Oh, Tamzin," Granddad said gently. "You weren't
sleeping – you were crying."

"It's silly, I know." I wanted to force a smile but my

face felt as though it would crack. "I think I've broken a rule – gotten too attached."

"And you don't want her to go," he said matter-of-factly. "Of course, I realize that. I've been trying to discuss it with Rosa's owners for some time but they've been away. They're back now."

I looked at him fearfully. "It's something horrible, isn't it? I can tell by your expression."

He nodded. "Yes it is. You know they told us they'd fired the groom who beat Rosa? Well, they've just discovered it wasn't the groom at all – it was their son, the son they bought Rosa for – he's the one who hurt her."

"But Mom said they were good people," I stammered. "She said –"

"I think they are. They're certainly not allowing the son to have anything more to do with horses, so of course they want me to sell Rosa. But I refused."

"What? But you can't let her go back there! You can't!"

"Tamzin," he held my shaking fingers. "I can't sell her because she's yours. Rosa is yours."

"You –" My heart was thudding so loudly I could hear it. "You bought her for me? But we only have other people's horses at Highfields! We don't have our own!"

"We do now." He reached out his other hand and patted the roan mare. "Rosa is yours, Tamzin, and it'll be nice for your dad's horse to have permanent company."

I hugged him so hard that he couldn't speak, and I think there were tears in his eyes too as he turned and left me to revel in my first day with my very own horse – Rosa, who'd never, ever again be a problem horse.

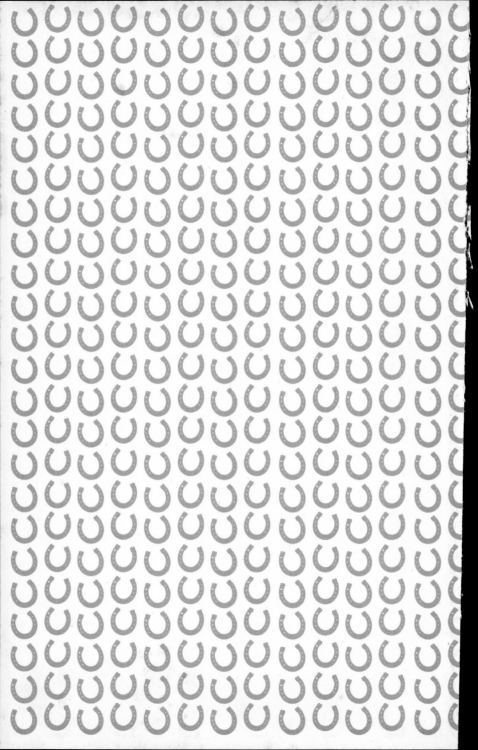